# The Embassy Ball

By John R. Teevan III

Author: John R. Teevan III

Cover photo & graphic design: John R. Teevan III

Albany, New York, USA

Printed by Kindle Direct Publishing

AuthorJohnTeevan@gmail.com

www.AuthorJohnTeevan.weebly.com

# A Note on the Date of Publication

I chose to publish *The Embassy Ball* on July 4th. Today is Independence Day – when writing and words and ideas and the signing of a document created an entire nation from the drawing boards. Just as the writing contained in this book creates new worlds from my imagination. Writing can start wars – as it did for the American Revolutionary War. Writing can make peace – as it did for the Treaty of Paris that ended it. Writing is not always perfect. But writing is beautiful and significant in that it lays the groundwork for thoughts to become reality. For dreams to come true. Writing is unique in that it embodies intangible thoughts and ideas onto tangible paper and ink. Or even electronic communication – text messages and emails and Kindle – transmit thoughts and ideas with electronic pulses in our technology just as our brains contemplate thoughts and ideas with electronic pulses between our neurons. Thoughts never really become tangible until they are written down. Once they are made tangible – once they are in written form – everything changes. You automatically own the copyright to new ideas once they are documented in tangible form. Once you sign a waiver you are legally bound by your signature. Once you sign a receipt you lose wealth. Once the Continental Congress signed the Declaration of Independence a new nation was born. I can't wait to see what happens after I publish this book.

JOHN R. TEEVAN III

# A Note on the Title

There are thirty-eight different stories that make up this collection. I could have chosen any one of them for the title of the collection. But I chose "The Embassy Ball." This holds a special place in my heart because I still remember fondly my first embassy ball. I met the Ambassador Extraordinary and Plenipotentiary of the Republic of Cameroon. We spoke in French in a register so formal that you only learn in school and use with ambassadors. One of my favorite movies is *My Fair Lady* where a linguist bets that he can teach a poor lady to speak so well that she can pass for royalty at an embassy ball. Well, that night I had my embassy ball. And I never forgot it. Entering the embassy we were transported into foreign territory. Legally we were in Cameroon – subject to Cameroonian law. And we really did feel like we were experiencing Cameroonian culture, surrounded by Cameroonian music, food and dance. But how could I be in Cameroon? I was in Washington, DC. Yet once I entered the embassy I was suddenly in an alternate universe. This will inspire any writer's imagination.

JOHN R. TEEVAN III

# Table of Contents

Professor Schneiderman's Discovery......1

Of Life and Death...........................5

The Writer and the Painter.................9

The State of the State of the Union........15

The Storm at Sea...........................21

A Note on The Storm at Sea..............25

Utopia.......................................27

The Photocopy Machine Repair
Technician...................................31

The Mayor of Strasbourg..................33

The New Pilot..............................37

The Chef....................................43

The *Mona Lisa* ...........................47

The Surgeon.................................49

The *Titanic*...............................53

The Embassy Ball..........................55

The French Revolution....................59

The DMV...................................61

The Translator...............................63

Harold Stresemann...........................65

The Actress.................................67

The Flemish Ambassador....................71

The Church Discovers that God is a
Woman.......................................77

The Maginot Line is Breached.............81

A Note on The Maginot Line is
Breached....................................85

Atomic Romance............................87

The Commissioner of Elections............91

Life Insurance...............................93

The Decision that Changed the World......95

The Life of a Superstar.......................99

The Freed Spirit............................107

The Office of Personnel Management.....109

The Pharmaceutical Salesman.............113

Luca Bianchi................................117

Dr. God.....................................125

The Berlin Wall.............................127

The Mechanic..............................131

Unwritten Rules............................133

Atomic Secrets...............................137

James's Long-Overdue Conversation......143

President McClellan...........................149

Bibliography...................................155

About the Author.............................157

Also by this Author...........................159

JOHN R. TEEVAN III

## Professor Schneiderman's Discovery

"Professor Schneiderman, where are you?"

"I'm in my office."

"No, I mean *where* are you?"

Suddenly, a mass of papers, books and maps shifted, revealing a bald but wise scholar – deep in thought, head in a cloud. Too busy thinking to get up from his desk so he just moved his papers so Captain Harrison could find him. Captain Harrison saw Professor Schneiderman in the gap in the pile of papers.

"Professor, have you found it?"

"I'm getting close. Don't interrupt me in the next four days. I'm on the verge of a breakthrough."

"But professor, you'll eat?"

"We are on the verge of finding the cure for cancer. So many lives are at stake. Eating will only take away my concentration."

"If you need food, let me know. Will you be going home tonight? Don't forget to sleep."

"The fate of thousands of lives are at stake. This is the cure to cancer we're talking about. One man's sleep is trivial."

"Yes, Professor Schneiderman. But *I* lose a lot of sleep over worrying about you."

"You are one man. You losing sleep over me is trivial compared to how many lives we will save with the cure for cancer."

"Professor, you've been trying to isolate the species in the rain forest that contains the cure for cancer for the last five years. Our grant ran out two years ago and I've been living on ramen noodles for the last two years. We need to start our expedition before our crew gives up on us. We can cure cancer – the fate of millions of lives are at stake – we just need you to finish the biochemistry research that will tell us where to go in the rainforest so we can extract the enzyme. This is all you, Professor Schneiderman. I believe in you."

Suddenly, inspiration struck. The numbers crunched. The gears turned. Professor Schneiderman jumped for joy. His hair stood on end in excitement – albeit only his nose hair and eyebrows. He was wise and bald. Papers flew around the office. Order and calmness did not describe the mental state – nor the chaotic office with papers flying around everywhere – of the man who had just discovered the cure for cancer.

"The picanese finches, found only in the Indonesian rain forest. Their bile produces the enzyme that sustains the great trees. Do you realize that? This tree – if you study its dendrochronology – has lived for 1,627 years. And if we didn't cut it down to date its tree rings it would have been immortal. Do you realize how old this tree is? This tree is older than my entire lifetime and yours combined."

"I'm not *that* old," Captain Harrison blushed.

"But I'm an old fart. This tree is old. 1,627 years. That's older than our entire country. That's older than the Declaration of Independence. Older than the Magna Carta. Older than Christopher Columbus's great grandfather's great grandfather. This tree would live on eternally. Humans could too, if our genes weren't predisposed to cancer. If nothing else kills us – heart attack, stroke – cancer will eventually do us in. This cure for cancer is also the secret to immortality! We shall now say I have isolated – and discovered – what shall henceforth be called the Schneiderman Enzyme. Just as this enzyme will allow people to live on forever, my name will live on forever with having discovered the Schneiderman Enzyme."

Captain Harrison – not wise and bald – but young, down-to-earth and practical, began preparations. "So where do we sail to in Indonesia?"

Professor Schneiderman provided the expedition's captain with the coordinates. "The Picanese finches breed here. We just need to extract their bile."

"Perfect. I'll make preparations and check the weather – I forget whether it will be summer or winter in Indonesia now."

Professor Schneiderman pointed to his globe. "Indonesia is on the equator. There *are* no seasons."

"Duly noted. I will gather our crew."

"Aye, aye, captain."

"I only hope we make enough money from the cure for cancer to pay our bills since the grant ran out two years ago. Two years of ramen noodles adds up."

Professor Schneiderman looked up from his books. "I just haven't eaten in two years. I can't concentrate on a full stomach. These were important calculations."

"Well, if our mission is successful, we won't just have a lifetime of happy eating – we'll have an eternity."

"Aye, aye, captain."

## Of Life and Death

Captain Harrison hesitated on taking the immortality potion. He was young and healthy but during their seventeenth expedition to Indonesia an accident occurred. A crate of picanese finches fell on his leg and crippled him. He was in much pain and would not be able to use his legs for the rest of his life.

"You can still take the immortality potion," Professor Schneiderman said. "Five centuries from now they'll have discovered a cure and you'll be able to walk again. Then you'll have the rest of eternity to enjoy."

Captain Harrison was not usually a deep thinker. But he pondered this intensely. Would five hundred years of pain and agony be worth an eternity of life? What if they don't find a cure for paralysis? And if he lives hundreds of years from now, who is to say that it won't just be a radioactive wasteland or a dystopia where he will suffer?

After careful reflection, Captain Harrison, an optimist, took the immortality potion. He couldn't abandon Professor Schneiderman – and a captain goes down with his ship. They would be buddies for the long haul. And taking this potion would be the most important science experiment of all time.

800 years went by.

The immortality potion was an amazing discovery. But their health deteriorated. Professor Schneiderman's teeth were falling out. Teeth decay slowly, but at age 879, your brown, rotting teeth look disgusting. He couldn't chew, so all he could eat was applesauce and mayonnaise. "Ew, that's disgusting," commented

Captain Harrison.

"No, not together. Separate."

"That's all you eat?"

"I've been eating nothing but applesauce and mayonnaise every day for 800 years. Life sucks!"

He couldn't bend or lift heavy objects because he had the back of an old man – an 879-year-old man. His metabolism slowed down so much over the years that he couldn't fit in his car's seat belt – and stopped flying because he was too obese to fit in an airplane seat. Professor Schneiderman wanted to die. He thought about this every day. But every time he attempted suicide, he would just do permanent damage to his body that he would be stuck in for all eternity. He was trapped on earth. His mind was brilliant – in the clouds – but the insanity of being chained to earth was driving him crazy.

The mad scientist promptly got to work. This time he wasn't trying to develop the immortality potion. He was finding the potion of death.

Ethically, he couldn't test on human subjects. It wouldn't be fair for them to die. So he drank every drug until he was so knocked out that he thought he was going to breathe his last.

"Captain Harrison, do me one last favor."

"Yes, professor."

"Set the picanese finches free. They deserve to live. And we deserve to die."

"Sometimes us dying seems like a privilege."

"It was a mistake to fabricate immortality potions. And those poor finches – we needed their bile to extract the enzymes. Set them free so no one else can be cursed with immortality."

"Yes, professor."

"Oh, and please, honor my wife."

"You're married?"

"She died. 827 years ago. It's tough to be widowed. But to grieve for 827 years … that was rough."

"Professor, I – I wish I could reassure you. I would say that you're gonna live, but I know that would be the last thing you'd ever want. I would say I hope you die, but that just sounds terrible. I – I don't really know what to say to you."

"Then don't say anything. Let me go quietly in peace. And I don't really have much to say myself. If I'd had something to say I'd have said it during my first 879 years. So now I go peacefully."

A picanese finch flew into Professor Schneiderman's arms. He petted it. And then let it fly free. At last, they were both in peace. The picanese finches were free to live and Professor Schneiderman was free to die.

JOHN R. TEEVAN III

## The Writer and the Painter

They met. The fateful encounter that changed their lives. The writer was late for a poetry open mic, shuffling papers through his briefcase to find his manuscript. He wasn't looking up and bumped into the painter, hidden behind a gigantic canvas and an even bigger easel with her hands full of bottles of toxic oil paints with pigments of every color. As they rounded the corner they collided. The writer's papers flew all over the hallway, and the painter's paint squirted all over his writing. She had left her mark on him.

"Oh, excuse me, I'm sorry, I didn't see you there."

"I'm so sorry. Here, let me help you pick up your papers." She bent over and saw the name on the manuscript. "Arthur O'Connor! Is that you?!"

"Yes."

"You're the bestselling author?!"

"Yes."

"Oh my god, what an honor. I – I – I don't really know what to say. I – I'm so humbled to meet you. I – "

"What's your name?"

"I – I – " She seemed to almost have forgotten her own name. She had just met a celebrity! But, alas, writers fall in love just as much as painters. And when the creative soul falls for someone, it falls hard. Writers and painters – all creative types – fall head-over-heels madly in love.

"I'm sorry, what did you say your name was?"

"Silvia."

"It's a pleasure to meet you."

"And an honor to meet you as well."

"Silvia, I have to get to my open mic. I'm doing a reading and I'm late. But here's my card. Keep in touch."

"And here's mine, sir."

"Arthur. Call me Arthur."

She melted with estrogen. Having picked up all of his papers, he closed his briefcase and headed off to the open mic.

"He'll probably forget me as soon as he leaves," thought Silvia.

But, alas. That evening she got an email. It was from Arthur O'Connor! He had her email address from her business card. But it was more than just an email. It was a love letter. As only a writer knows how to pour his heart and soul into writing. She could not help but fall in love with him as she read each word. It was like a romance novel – only not fiction, it was about her and Arthur! This love letter was the best email she had ever received – and the liveliest two pages of nonfiction she had ever read.

So what did she do?

An artist creates, and she was a painter. So she painted a glorious, glamorous portrait of her favorite author.

"Dear Arthur," she typed in the email, "I have a painting I'd like to give to you. But it's too big to mail. I guess we'll just have to meet. It's a date?"

Six months later the painter and the writer were still together. They loved each other as if they had met yesterday. The passions of a creative soul – be it a painter or a writer – are stronger than a magnet attracted to its opposite pole. He wrote bestselling novels and she illustrated them. Their lives – their passions – their creativity – intertwined. They were artists, and they worked together as a dynamic duo. The writer often published romance novels and there was always a character whose personality and beauty and creativity and charm identically resembled Silvia. But it couldn't be her, of course, since the characters were not named Silvia. One must respect the ethics of writing about real people. You cannot include real people as characters in your book. So Arthur changed the name and kept Silvia in every one of his books. Likewise, Silvia always had one person in the crowd in all of her masterpieces that resembled Arthur perfectly. He never posed for her – she knew what he looked like even with her eyes closed. She dreamed about him every day. Keeping him in her paintings was her way of being reminded of the love in her life.

Until it happened. When you're a famous writer, you have fangirls on four continents. Book signings and selfies with the bestselling author often lead to after-hours drinks and literary agent introductions and networking that borders on flirting. And then it happened. Arthur cheated on Silvia.

"I'm sorry, Silvia. I messed up. I'm trying to tell you and be honest with you about my mistake – "

"Who was it?"

"I – I don't know her name. Silvia, I have 45,692 followers on Instagram. I have fangirls on four continents. I can't keep track of 'em all. I don't know her name. Just know that it meant nothing."

But Silvia was heartbroken. Her soulmate had betrayed her.

For a nameless fangirl. There was only one thing she could do to get revenge. Cheat on him with as many guys as she could convince to fall in love with her tonight at the bar downtown. Every man she went home with was out of spite for Arthur, not actual love. The emotions of an artist run deep. And vengeance seems all-consuming.

The writer began publishing novels about a vengeful slut. Silvia was no longer the protagonist of his stories but now the lowlife who everyone shamed. Silvia retaliated by painting – splattering oil on canvas with the fire and fury of an enraged artist – and painting Arthur as ugly, decrepit and villainous.

Finally, they regained an even keel. Thirty years passed. They did not talk. They had not seen each other, yet somehow longed for the past.

The writer was shuffling papers in his briefcase, looking for his manuscript, late for his book talk. The painter was rushing to the oil painting class she was teaching, with canvas on gigantic easel covering her face and bottles of toxic oil paints with pigments of every color in her arms. They collided on the corner of the hallway in the arts center, the same corner where they first met. Both stared in disbelief. Then smiled.

"Silvia, I – "

"Arthur, I'm sorry I didn't see you. I – um, what are you doing here?"

"I'm doing an author's talk for my new book. And you?"

"I'm teaching an oil painting class."

The writer looked down. He looked up, peering deep into Silvia's beautiful brown eyes. He looked down at his watch.

"My publisher will be there. My agent is organizing my book

signing. I'm late, it started – "

The writer paused. For a man of words, for once in his life he had no words to think of. He was speechless.

"I'm sorry, I should let you go."

"No, Silvia, wait. I want to tell you something. I love you. I – "

She approached him and kissed him.

"Silvia, I have 440 tickets sold for my author's talk today. 440 paying fans waiting to see me right now. But they don't matter. I'll skip the reading. Seeing you means it all for me. Would you like to get a coffee at the – "

"Yes."

"I could accompany you to your class if you'd like to – "

"Screw the class. Arthur, you're the love of my life. The painting class can go without an instructor. They'll just paint abstract art – a five-year-old could paint that."

So the two lovers, at last reunited, spent the afternoon catching up – and falling in love all over again.

Finally, six hours late, Arthur arrived at his author's talk.

His agent approached him. "Arthur, where have you been? We were wondering if we would have to refund a full house! What – "

"Derek, let me introduce you to Silvia, the love of my life. Those six hours were used to unlock my writer's block. I'm now inspired to write another ten novels. A love story."

The agent shook his head. "I'll never understand writers."

Arthur walked up the steps of the stage. A crowd of hundreds of fans cheered. He asked Silvia to come up too and take a chair beside him on stage.

"Who's this?" asked his publisher.

"She's my illustrator. We have some amazing books in the works together. I write and she does the artwork. To my readers who liked my books so far, I can assure you that the best is yet to come."

## The State of the State of the Union

The State of the Union was today. Thousands of people – nationwide – worldwide – turned on their TVs to watch the speech. Every year the most important day in the House Chamber was when the President made his annual address to Congress. The Vice President was there. The Senate Majority Leader, the Secretary of State, the Speaker of the House – they all took their seats to watch – to listen to – the President as he laid out his agenda for the next year.

The State of the Union is the only day when the public cannot walk in and attend a session of Congress. Every seat is taken, and security is at a record high. Two houses of Congress try to squeeze into a chamber that only fits one house of Congress. Space is limited, so only important, high-level government officials get invited. The President went through more agony when deciding who to send invitations to for his State of the Union than he did when deciding who to invite to his wedding.

Speaking of the President, here he comes. The moment we've all been waiting for. The President approached the podium. All 435 Congressmen and 100 Senators and cabinet members were immediately silent. Nobody would interrupt the President of the United States of America. Not a Governor. Not a policeman. Not a Senator. Even the flies went silent. There were hundreds of cell phones in that room – some Senators had three cell phones each – but every single cell phone was turned off. Nothing would interrupt the President's speech. The President opened his mouth to begin his address.

"Rang! Rang! Rang!" The fire alarm went off.

The President looked for the Sergeant-at-Arms, in charge of securing the House chamber.

"Where is the Sergeant-at-Arms?" the President called out.

A man emerged from the crowd.

"What the hell is going on?" the President demanded.

"Mr. President, it appears that we've violated the fire code. Our room is over capacity. This chamber was meant to fit enough people to host the House of Representatives – not the House of Representatives and the Senate and the cabinet and photographers and the press and – "

"But what the hell do we do about it?"

"It will take a while for maintenance to find out exactly which fire alarm was pulled. In the meantime, the building could be on fire. For our safety – for our government – for our nation – for our people – we must protect the lives of the important leaders in this room. We need to evacuate the Capitol. It is a fire alarm, after all, and that's what you do when the fire alarm goes off. You exit the building."

The Director of the Secret Service was on his radio, desperately communicating with his officers with panic in his eyes. The President looked at him and asked, "Will we have enough security for all of our most important government officials to all be outside on the National Mall with god knows who else is walking around on that public lawn?"

"It would be safer if we went out the way we came in. Through the tunnels. That will get us far away to safety," said the Director of the Secret Service.

"What?!" interrupted the Sergeant-at-Arms. "Send our

nation's most important leaders down deeper into a burning building?! That's absurd! We should follow the emergency exit signs and exit the building to get away from the fire."

The fire alarm was still piercing with a high-pitched sound so annoying that the President finally said, "Let's get outta here. This noise is hurting my ears. Ladies and gentlemen, please exit the building. We will reconvene on the National Mall. It's stuffy in here and we could all use some fresh air."

"But Mr. President!" objected the Director of the Secret Service.

"I'm the President," he reminded. "I preside over everyone in this room – everyone in this nation. My decision is that we will follow the established procedures for a fire drill instead of go deeper into a building that could be on fire. Your job, as Director of the Secret Service, is to secure the premises. And I advise that you do it soon because we're leaving now."

The Director of the Secret Service looked like he was going to have a stroke or shit his pants or have a heart attack – or all three at the same time. Every significant member of the government was going to be on the National Mall – the lawn outdoors that was open to the public – in just a few moments. It would be any anarchist's dream. One sniper hidden in the Washington Monument opens fire and America falls into chaos. The President is dead.

But the Constitution provides a back-up. If the President, the Vice President, the Speaker of the House, the President pro tempore of the Senate – all standing next to each other on the National Mall, outdoors in public – if something happens and they all get wiped out, the laws of succession protect us. They tell us who will be our leader and prevent power struggles in a crisis that would be chaotic enough.

The Secret Service had planned for this scenario with succession in mind. Before the speech, the cabinet members drew straws and one of them was sent to Seattle, far away from Washington, DC in case a nuclear missile wiped out the entire speech's attendance.

The only person in line for succession who wasn't in the crowd on the National Mall – the crowd that could easily be gunned down by a machine gun hanging out the window of a car passing by – the crowd that could easily be destroyed by a single bomb hidden in the grass beneath the National Mall – the only person in line for succession who wasn't there was the Secretary of Agriculture. Can you believe it? If all hell breaks loose, the most powerful nation in the world being led by … a farmer?!

The leaders gathered in the National Mall right outside the Capitol. Ironically, they were all standing around the Garfield Monument, which honors President Garfield who was assassinated. Would the same thing happen today? Would the President be shot? Only this time with the entire cabinet, Senate and House of Representatives with him?

But alas, everything worked out. For all of the fears of anarchy and presidential assassinations, none of the fears running thorough the mind of the Director of the Secret Service were true. In fact, it turned out to be nice outdoors. Rather than the stuffy chamber, the weather outside was beautiful. The sunlight from outdoors combined with the majestic Capitol in the background resulted in many amazing photos captured by the photographers during the speech. And for the first time in the history of our nation, hundreds and hundreds and hundreds of citizens gathered to witness their very first State of the Union speech – now open to the public – because there was much more room outdoors.

So what caused the fire alarms? It wasn't an anarchist trying to get the politicians to exit the building so they could be gunned down. It turns out that one of the fire alarms was just accidentally set off. The alarm was bumped by a curator who was removing a Confederate statue of Robert E. Lee from the Capitol Rotunda. Those things are anchored down well after many years of rust. She tugged and tugged. When the statue suddenly gave way the curator fell back and bumped the fire alarm. And then the famous Evacuation Affair started, interrupting the State of the Union Speech.

At first everyone hated the curator for having made the nation fear a government takeover and a violent assassination of the entire government. But years later everyone began to thank her. It was because of her that the State of the Union was henceforth outdoors – with enough seats so ordinary citizens could spectate. The presidential photographers took better pictures with the sunlight. The President enjoyed the fresh air that made him give better speeches.

And the curator became a national hero for starting the tradition of hosting the State of the Union address outdoors.

JOHN R. TEEVAN III

## The Storm at Sea

The storm at sea. The waves crashed and the wind howled with all the fury and passion of an enraged tyrant. Will the boat sink? Will there be survivors? Or will this be the end for the brave sailors on board?

The sailors, in a panic, turned to their captain.

"He's not available now. He's doing his last prayers," said the first mate.

Hope was gone. Luck had run out. The poor sailors would meet their end.

A gigantic wave came crashing down on the boat. Ka-boom! The boat was shattered. The men who knew how to swim swam for their lives. Those who didn't perished.

Of the crew of one hundred sailors, only twenty survived and made it to the island. Where were they? The navigator disappeared in the shipwreck. Without his compass the entire crew was lost.

It is during these times when we are completely lost that we find ourselves.

Yes, there was plenty of fear. But in a sense the crew was free. Society with its strict rules – they were on an island all alone, free from the laws and the social expectations and all of the other restrictions society imposes. They were liberated. The captain, who ruled with an iron fist, was dead. So now the sailors were free. What new social order will they create on this island of paradise where freedom flows like water from the streams?

The void after the tyrannical control of the past can create either freedom or anarchy. Or both at the same time.

"As first mate, I should assume control," Yves announced.

"No, Yves. You are of the past. We are freed from the chains of the past. The captain is dead. Finally we are free. Down with the tyrants of the past!" Jules proclaimed.

"So it's a mutiny?"

"Not a mutiny. A revolution."

"So it's treason."

"It wasn't our doing to break down the system. God – destiny – freed us and led us to this island. And God gave us our innate freedoms and our natural rights that the captain took away from us. Finally we have the opportunity to win back our freedom. Down with the tyrants!"

The sailors shouted in support of Jules. They encircled Yves.

"Treason! Mutiny!" Yves shouted.

"We choose freedom. Down with the tyrant!" proclaimed Jules.

"Don't touch me!" Yves shouted as he took out his revolver.

The crowd, in self defense, massacred Yves. The first act of the new order was a murder. Sometimes one must cut ties with the past in order to create something new.

"I take it upon myself to lead our new nation," Jules

announced and the crowd rejoiced. "I'll be the President. You, Leon, you can be Vice President. Phil, you'll be chef."

"But, but I'm only a cook."

"It was always your dream to become a chef, wasn't it?"

"Yes, of course."

"Today we are cutting ties with the past. You have all the training of a chef. Before, on the boat, you were limited to being only a cook. But today you are free. Your dream has come true. Congratulations. You are now a chef. Now go cook us a nutritious and delicious meal to feed the masses. I believe in you. And your nation depends on you. We need you to be a chef. Phil, this is your moment to shine."

And Phil was the best chef in the entire Indian Ocean.

The carpenter built houses. The fishermen fished fresh fish. The colony lived on the island in peace. Everyone prospered. And freedom flowed like water from the streams.

All of a sudden, a search and rescue boat reached the island. "Oh! Sorry it took us so long to find you. The weather was terrible with zero visibility and we weren't sure if there were any survivors from your ship that sank. Finally! Thank god we found you. Come with me, I'll take you back to Nantes. I'm sure you're dying to come home."

Leon, the Vice President, looked at Jules, the President. Jules nodded.

They didn't want to leave their island of paradise. They paid off the search and rescue crew who returned to France.

"We didn't find anyone," they reported to Paris.

And the sailors lived on the island of paradise, free and in peace.

## A Note on The Storm at Sea

*I titled this piece "The Storm at Sea" because that was the act of God that shook things up and created the new world order for the sailors. Change comes slowly to those who work for progress. Sometimes we have to shake things up a bit to get to paradise. And when the rescue crew comes to return us to our harsh reality, we may not want to leave.*

*But why did they prosper on the island? They should have starved, cut off from society with only twenty men. But we can learn from their success. Those who were good at cooking became chefs. Those who were good at building became carpenters. There was no favoritism or political considerations or social pressures based on inherited social standing. When your survival depends on it and you are on a deserted island, you maximize all of the resources and talents so everyone can contribute to the best of their abilities for the survival of the collective.*

*There may have been historical inspiration for the names. The President, Jules, could be named after the four Jules who founded the Third Republic in France: Jules Ferry, Jules Favre, Jules Simon and Jules Grévy. Jules, as all four of them happened to be named, built democracy in modern France, just as Jules in this story develops democracy on the island. As Emperor Napoléon III's dictatorship falls, just as the captain's reign ends, Jules creates a new system that is democratic and beneficial to all. Léon, his Vice President, could have been inspired by Léon Blum, the first socialist Prime Minister in France. We can see the themes of a revolution: the people occupying the powers that once oppressed them for the benefit of the collective – the proletariat – without the tyranny of the oppressor, be it the captain or Hitler or the bourgeoisie.*

*My question to you, the reader, is: what will your role be on the island? What are your talents? What can you contribute to this world? And once you join this utopia, would you ever want to leave?*

*This story was originally written in French. As with any translation, the original text always contains the purest, most articulate expression of ideas that are fresh and creative and not lost in translation. However, I wanted to translate it to English so all readers could access it.*

## Utopia

"Ships on the horizon, sir."

"How many?"

"Seventeen warships."

"What flag?"

"France."

Sometimes it is easier to fight your enemies than to face yourself. An enemy warship can easily be destroyed without any guilt. But facing your own reality – with all of your country's complex social problems – it's hard to not get sucked in and let your own emotions get in the way. You cannot conquer something you are already a part of. Or are they? The sailors lived in isolation on this deserted island in the Indian Ocean, far away from the despots in Paris. They prospered beyond measure. And now their utopia had been discovered.

The first boat landed on the island. The sailors living on the island came to meet the intruders.

As two more boats landed, the ship's captain took out handcuffs.

"In the name of his majesty the emperor of France, you are under arrest."

"What for?" demanded Jules.

"For mutiny, desertion and murder."

Jules paused.

"Well, for mutiny, we had no choice. Our captain was dead. So we couldn't follow his orders. We had to organize on our own.

"For desertion, our capsized ship brought us here. We didn't flee France. We were stuck on this island by no choice of our own. The storm brought us here.

"As for murder, well, we are a new social order. How many people died when the French nation formed? And in the French Revolution? And the Reign of Terror? And the Napoleonic Wars? And the bloodshed in the Revolution of 1848? And – "

"You killed Yves Bouchard."

"We had to. It was either our survival or his. We would all suffer if he lived. Our new nation depended on it. Likewise, how many Frenchmen died in the guillotine during the French Revolution? Individual deaths are an unfortunate but necessary casualty of nation-building."

"Look, Jules, I don't need your philosophical manifestos. The emperor has spared your life. I'm not going to kill you. You should be grateful for the mercy being afforded to you. You killed a man and your life is spared. Now get in these handcuffs. I'm taking you to the political prison in New Caledonia."

Jules looked at the seven other row boats that had just reached shore, each filled with a dozen soldiers with muskets and capes and képis. His men on the island were outnumbered ten to one.

Jules sighed. "Well, let me at least give you a tour of the island first. That way you'll know what you're missing when you row me out of here."

"What do you mean?" asked the captain.

"This island is paradise. A functional utopia. You see that housing complex over there?"

"Yes."

"Two carpenters built that."

"That entire suburb was built by two men?"

"Building was their passion. Now that they're free from the pressure of their family's expectations and the social class restrictions and corrupt laws that prevent them from getting their building licenses – "

"Hey!" interjected the captain, "I was Building Code Commissioner in Bordeaux! I issued those licenses."

"Yes, and you see, now you won't need bribes to issue professional licenses. Now politics won't bog you down. You can do whatever you want," proclaimed Jules.

"I always did want to be a painter," admitted the captain.

"Then let me show you the most beautiful view of the sunrise on the cliffs. Come with me."

"But, but – but my ship. We're supposed to arrest you and take you to prison in New Caledonia."

"Then just stay here," Jules replied.

"I wish I could. I've never felt so free. So happy. Like I could reach my dreams."

"Then here's what we'll do." Jules whispered plans in the captain's ear.

The ship returned to France. The crew was told to say that

they did not find the island. And that the captain died at sea. But he did not die – he was reborn. The captain lived a long and happy life in utopia on the island of paradise. He became a painter and award-winning artist and most of all he became happier than he ever was before. And Jules was not handcuffed and sent to political prison in New Caledonia. Everyone prospered on the island with their freedom. Their talents went to good use, free from society's restrictions and expectations. And the men lived in peace on this island of utopia.

## The Photocopy Machine Repair Technician

"I heard Nicole got a new boyfriend."

"Really? What's he like?"

"Is he cute?"

"Is he funny?"

"Is he rich?"

"Actually, he's a photocopy machine repair technician."

A brief pause. Then the girls all unanimously agreed: "Wow, she's lucky. I wish I had one like that. He's a keeper!"

The photocopy machine is what unites coworkers in every office. More specifically, hatred for copier jams and temperamental machines that seem to break just when you need them the most. In an office full of blacks and whites and Asians and Christians and Muslims and atheists and Jews and rednecks and millennials and almost-retired baby boomers and workers from every department within the office, the only thing that unites them all is their hatred for the copy machine and its many paper jams. And a photocopy repair technician will go far. Nicole was now the most popular friend as she walked into the break room.

"Can Kyle come to work today?"

"We'd love to meet him."

"No, he should come to *our* office first. Our photocopy

machine has been down for six days."

"No, I get first dibs. My copy machine is older than yours. We haven't gotten an upgrade in eight years. If it breaks while he's here, he'll roll up his sleeves and reveal his muscular biceps – "

"You guys! Kyle and I broke up on Saturday."

"Oh. Damn."

"Our machine really did need a tune-up. Too bad."

"Nicole, we'll have to postpone that meeting regarding your promotion."

"I guess our department will have to allocate more funds for hiring a technician."

Nicole looked down. So much for friends helping her through a break-up.

## The Mayor of Strasbourg

"Alsace is neither France nor Germany. Too many world wars have been fought over this tiny strip of land. We are finally settling the issue once and for all. Alsace is, and henceforth shall be, an independent republic," proclaimed the Mayor of Strasbourg.

News hit the papers. The German kaiser and the French premier were shocked. "Well this was unexpected."

The generals and colonels pushed for war. A quick and easy invasion to annex the territory and claim it as their own.

"Wait, we can't do that."

"Why not?"

"Because European Parliament meets in Strasbourg. Any attack on neutral territory will have all of Europe up in arms against us."

"You're right. The European Commission would turn against us. So what do we do?"

"General, there's a way of waging war that is and always has been more effective than violence. Economic warfare. We boycott all items made in Alsace until they return to us. A complete embargo. They'll be on their knees to come back before we can even forget them."

"Perfect. We'll begin the movement at once."

Germany and France both organized embargoes against Alsace. But soon they were the ones who suffered. Because Alsace produces the best wine.

"Those damned Alsatians! How I miss their wine. And now Alsace wine is going on the black market for five times the price! This is only helping the Alsatian economy, not hurting it!"

"We must rethink Plan B."

"Bribes! We must give them a better incentive to come to France than to join Germany."

"Yes, of course. I'd say € 15 million."

"€ 150 million. It's really good wine, and I wouldn't want the Germans to get the vineyards."

The French leadership agreed to cut a check in that amount.

At the next cabinet meeting in Paris, they developed a plan. The French Prime Minister explained to his Minister of Foreign Affairs, "Georges, it should be Jacques who goes, not you. It gives the wrong message. If the Minister of the Interior goes to Strasbourg then it reinforces that Alsace is and always was a part of France. If the Minister of Foreign Affairs goes, then it implies that Alsace is a foreign country independent from France."

"Yes, but I really like Alsace wine. We really need them back. If I go as Minister of Foreign Affairs, it will give them what they want in dignifying their sovereignty movement. That might make them more amenable to coming back. And I really want them back. I love their wine."

"Alright, you idiot. *I'll* go. If the Prime Minister takes time from his busy schedule to show up, it will flatter them. And it avoids the whole Interior/Foreign Affairs dilemma."

"Great. And if I'm not going, could you bring me back some

– "

"I'll bring back a bottle of Alsace wine for you, don't worry."

The French Prime Minister met with the Mayor of Strasbourg. A price was offered. € 150 million if Alsace would return to France.

"I am sorry, monsieur, but the Germans are offering us € 175 million."

"What?! They won't win this war. We'll give you € 200 million if you return today."

They shook hands.

As the French Prime Minister was leaving, the Deputy Mayor of Strasbourg turned to the Mayor and whispered, "Did he really just give us € 200 million?"

"I told you this strategy would work. Pretend to leave, they bribe you to come back, and suddenly our city's treasury is swimming in money! We didn't even have to do anything and just got paid € 200 million."

And they toasted to their success with glasses of the finest Alsace wine.

JOHN R. TEEVAN III

# The New Pilot

The Deputy Commissioner of Education looked at his watch. Only six more hours until his plane lands in London. He was on his way to a conference. He loved professional development. Getting paid and you don't have to go to work. Instead you get a free flight to Europe with hotel and per diem paid for by … well, by the taxpayers who pay his state salary. He reclined his seat and closed his eyes to take a nap. Just as he was falling asleep … boom! The plane shook. Like they had hit something. What was it? Suddenly, the plane took a nose dive. They were losing altitude. One of the engines was out. Another boom. The Deputy Commissioner looked behind himself. The plane was on fire! Another explosion rocked the plane. And the plane spiraled downward. The passengers panicked. Everyone was getting up as the flight attendants told everyone to stay in their seats, brace for landing and remain calm. The Deputy Commissioner made his way to the front of the plane.

"What happened?" he asked the flight attendant.

"We've been struck three times by anti-aircraft shells."

"From who?"

"Iceland."

"What?!"

"Brexit has been rescinded. The European Union recently re-admitted England. England fought a war to maintain their control over the U.S. We may have won our revolution, but England still

37

holds a grudge. Their voice resoundingly criticizes us in Brussels. And America has no representation in EU Parliament. So since we're flying over EU territory now, Iceland shot us down. We're an enemy to their EU clique."

"WTF?!"

"Anyhow, we're going to crash any moment now. Our engine has been shot down. We probably won't live to see tomorrow."

"But, but, um, the pilot, couldn't he land us in the ocean?"

"The pilot took the parachute and ejected himself. You can see him out the window slowly landing on the ocean."

"Where are the other parachutes?"

"Um, the copilot took the other one."

"Is there anyone else on this plane who can land us in the ocean so we don't all die from impact?"

The flight attendant sighed. "There's no way in hell that we're going to make it out alive. The reality is that everyone on this plane is going to die in a few minutes. Would you rather have them die in peace and tell them 'keep calm'? Or would you rather torture them on their last moments of life by asking on the loud speaker, 'Does anyone know how to fly a plane?'? It will only make them panic and ruin their last few moments of life."

The Deputy Commissioner sighed. These are the important decisions he has to ponder every day. When a student gets mumps, does he tell everyone and make them panic? Or does he not tell them? The student was treated and is not contagious anymore. So why does the law require him to make a public announcement? After all, he *is* the law. And his judgement is more appropriate for each situation than archaic writing filed in the state archives of legal guidelines. The Deputy Commissioner sighed.

"How about this. I'll fly the plane. Nobody will find out that we don't have a pilot. None of the passengers will panic. I'll land us and we'll be saved."

"Sometimes a quick and painless death on impact is better than smacking down on the water with all of us on board being paralyzed and living the rest of our lives in wheelchairs with fractured spines."

"Do you want to land this plane?"

The flight attendant shook her head.

The Deputy Commissioner entered the cockpit and took control of the joystick.

"This is the throttle. I wonder if that'll make us go faster so we can regain our altitude."

He pulled the throttle. Suddenly a loud sound of an engine burning up, and then the fire of the engine exploding, and then the engine fell off the nose of the plane.

"Well, that didn't help."

Suddenly: Bang! Bang! Bang! A fighter plane was firing at their plane. "Does anybody have a fire arm with them?" the Deputy Commissioner asked on the loud speaker.

"I do."

"I do."

"Me too."

"I have three automatic machine guns in my carry-on."

"What?!" asked the Deputy Commissioner, "You got three automatic machine guns through airport security?"

"We're Americans. Of *course* we have guns. I carry my gun with me everywhere I go. Even on airplanes. Second Amendment – it's in our Constitution."

There are times when the Deputy Commissioner is proud to lead Americans. And other times when it's just plain embarrassing to govern them.

"We're under fire from the fighter plane to the right. Can you return fire?" he asked.

"I sure as hell can. I'm from Texas. The only form of gun control we have in Texas is aiming straight. Controlling your gun – that's gun control in Texas!"

"Open fire!" proclaimed the Deputy Commissioner.

Bam! Bam! Bam! Soon the Icelandic fighter plane was crashing into the ocean.

"Does everyone know how to swim?"

The passengers nodded.

"Put on your life vests."

"Will it be cold? Should I wear my coat? I hear it's freezing out."

"Yes, but we might land in an Icelandic hot spring. So be

prepared for hot tub temperatures."

And they crashed into the Atlantic and all of them survived and had a pool party.

"I don't think we should swim to shore. Iceland is hostile territory. We might get shot. I think we should swim back to New York."

"Um, I don't think I can do that. I can only tread water for two minutes."

"That's ok. You won't be treading water. You'll be swimming."

"For eighteen hours."

"Right. Swimming. Not treading water. So you'll be fine."

"But I've never swam for eighteen hours."

"Well, you'll get a good workout in."

And they all swam back to New York. And they made records as Olympic athletes in swimming.

JOHN R. TEEVAN III

# The Chef

"Soufflée, sautée, coq au vin, fillet mignon – "

"I'm sorry, sir, I don't speak French."

"But you're a cook. You should know these things."

"I'm the cook. You're the chef. You know the fancy French words. I just boil water."

The chef scratched his head. "How do you even feed yourself? You incompetent idiot, you can't even cook! How do you feed yourself?"

"I'm the #1 customer at our restaurant. I buy breakfast, lunch and dinner here. I never have to cook. Our owner likes it because I patronize our business. And I can give recommendations on what's good on the menu – because I've had everything on the menu at least three times each."

"So why did the owner hire you as a cook? You don't even know how to cook!"

"I was here every day all day taking up space at the bar for all of my meals. So he figured, why not put me to work? I boil water for him and he gets me off the bar stool."

"You are an idiot."

"Actually, I'm a genius. Because now I can snack on all of my meals all day long in the kitchen for free. And I get paid doing it."

JOHN R. TEEVAN III

"What you're doing is wrong, but I'll give you this: you're a genius. Teach me how to game the system."

"Well, for starters, you have to go from a good chef to a crappy chef."

"What do you mean?"

"Make soup. Pretend that it's terrible. Too much salt. You can't serve it to customers. It has to be discarded. Now you have lunch for a week."

"But – "

"There ain't no such thing as a free lunch. No one's gonna *give* you a free lunch. You have to *take* it."

"But that's stealing."

"Jean-Philippe, how much of the pot of soup will be thrown out and wasted anyway?"

"Um, probably the whole pot, unless a customer or two orders the soup."

"So you're being responsible by not wasting food. Every time food gets thrown out, the price of food rises and the starving poor in Third World Countries – "

"Bill, we can't just pocket all of the owner's food. That wouldn't be fair to him."

"But think of the starving poor – "

"You know what? There's only one place where incompetent lazy chefs who don't know how to cook can get hired – and promoted. And that's the civil service. I say we help the poor and feed the hungry at the soup kitchen."

"And we'll get state employee benefits!"

"And we can steal food from the soup kitchen and we'll never get fired because government jobs are protected!"

And they got jobs at the soup kitchen and never went hungry again. Jean-Philippe cooked a delicious soup – with a bit too much salt – and there was enough to go around. Especially for Bill and Jean-Philippe.

JOHN R. TEEVAN III

# The *Mona Lisa*

"Your royal majesty, why should we invade Italy? We just fought a Hundred Years' War. Our men are exhausted. Why another bloody, destructive war?"

The king of France scratched his head. "I really like the *Mona Lisa*. Da Vinci's painting is in Florence. I'm an art collector and this would enlarge my royal collection – and glorify our kingdom."

"A war over one painting?"

"It's a masterpiece! Someday the *Mona Lisa* will be famous."

"But right now it's just oil on canvas gathering dust in a foreign country. I do not think we should invade Italy and start a war."

The king of France sighed. "Art inspires imagination. Creativity solves the world's problems. This *Mona Lisa* – is she smiling? – art has the same meaning no matter what language it is in. Poetry and government proclamations make no sense once we cross the border. But art unites humanity."

"And art kills humanity. People will die for this painting if you start a war."

The king of France scratched his head. "Louis, the arts – culture – theater – painting – writing – performance – drawing – dance – they enlighten the world. They give meaning to our otherwise mundane existence."

"But – "

"When we plunder Florence, we will bring back the Renaissance. Da Vinci's paintings will be on display in the Louvre. And the fleur-de-lis will forever be in Florence's coat-of-arms."

"Wait, we'll infiltrate their flag?"

"Launch the invasion today and history is ours."

Louis, the soldier, had no appreciation for art. But leaving his mark on a coat of arms was like conquering a nation and parading through their capital. "Your royal majesty, I'm in!"

"We shall commence the attack tonight under the cover of darkness."

"And tomorrow Florence is ours!"

"And the fleur-de-lis will be on their flag for all eternity!"

"And I will get the *Mona Lisa* for all eternity!"

The soldier shrugged, muttered to himself, "whatever," and planned the attack.

Florence was overtaken. And the king of France plundered and looted Italy. The fleur-de-lis was engraved onto the flag of Florence – and remains there today. The king of France gloriously brought back to Paris the wealth and gold and art of Florence. Including the *Mona Lisa*.

# The Surgeon

"Doctor, where are you going?"

"I'll be back."

"But the operation starts in 30 minutes."

"So the patient will be better off without me cutting him open and all the drugs and side effects and risks of the surgery. He will be better off without my knife in his belly."

"But we already gave him the anesthesia."

"Perfect. He's asleep. When he wakes up, tell him that we did the operation. The placebo is always more effective than medicine. You feel better without the side effects."

"But that's dishonest!"

"The patient asked us to treat his illness. And I did exactly that. What he doesn't know won't hurt him."

"But the anesthesia is expensive. The health insurance company won't pay you anything if there're no surgery."

The doctor sighed. "They pay me enough – they pay me too much – I am richer than a gold mine. They pay me enough to put bread on the table. All I really need is the copay. The rest – greed is a sin."

"But it's the difference between $20 and $9,859.01. That's a big difference – and a lot of money!"

"Henry, when you are my age, you will understand that time is more valuable than money. I'd really like to pocket an extra $9,859.01. But my time is more valuable. The train leaves in 45 minutes. And life doesn't wait for anyone."

"Where will you go?"

The doctor sighed. "Life takes you where destiny brings you. I bought a one-way ticket. First South, then West, and I'll end up wherever the wind takes me."

"But who will take your place in the hospital?"

"You. Congratulations. I'm promoting you to take my position."

"But I'm just a nurse! I'm not a doctor!"

Dr. Rousseau handed Henry his scrubs, the white jacket with his name and M.D. embroidered on it.

"It says 'Dr. Rousseau.' You'll do fine in my place. Just wear the scrubs and everyone will think you're a doctor."

"But I don't know anything! I have no training –"

"Yes you do! Nurses have a training just as much as doctors have a training. And both trainings are useless. It's experience that is worth more, anyway."

"But I've never done surgery!"

"So you should thank me for this opportunity to gain more experience."

"But – but – I won't know what to do! I never attended med school! I'm a nurse, not a doctor!"

"Nurses, doctors, they're all the same. We help patients. And, for both doctors and nurses, we are nothing without experience. So I'm giving you an experience you can put on your résumé. You'll thank me for it later."

"But when they discover that I don't know – that I'm not a doctor…"

"Henry, after two days wearing my scrubs, you will be rich enough to pay your bills for the rest of your life. And if – or more likely *when* – they find out, well, you can escape like me. Buy a one-way ticket. South, then West, and soon we'll be having a beer together in Hawaii."

And the doctor left, leaving his scrubs in Henry's hands. He took the train South, then West, with his one-way ticket to wherever destiny brings him.

JOHN R. TEEVAN III

# The *Titanic*

"Captain, we've sprung a leak!"

"Can we plug it?"

"We're trying everything we can. We're stuffing all of our crew's clothing – everything that we can find – anything that we're not wearing – into the hole to try and plug it."

"And?"

"We're taking in water fast. The clothes get wet and weigh our boat down."

"You mean?"

"Yup. Just like the *Titanic*. I'd say we have about three hours before this ship is completely underwater."

"Quick! Ready the lifeboats! We'll escape that way."

"'We'? My dear captain, you would live with dishonor for the rest of your life! The captain goes down with his ship."

The captain paused. His first mate had just given him a death sentence. Either die today in the cold waters of the Baltic Sea. Or die a thousand deaths of shame and dishonor for abandoning ship. Which is worse? As Shakespeare writes, "A coward dies a thousand times before his death, but the valiant taste of death but once." How can he escape alive?

"Bob! You're chewing gum."

"Oh, sorry, captain. I meant to spit this out. I'll spit this out now. Sorry." And he took a handkerchief, brought it to his mouth and then was about to throw the handkerchief with gum overboard.

"No! No, don't!" The captain tackled his first mate.

"What – wha – are you mad?"

"Our very lives depend on this. Don't throw out that gum."

"What do you mean?"

The captain took the gum and plugged the hole in the boat. The gum expanded – like someone blowing bubblegum. But the ship was able to make it back to harbor without sinking. And the captain and his crew made it back. Every man alive.

"Well, that ended better than *Titanic*."

"Actually, I kind of like the movie's ending. It's a beautiful, sad, sweet love story and – "

"Then next time you're the captain."

"Better keep gum on me at all times."

# The Embassy Ball

It was love at first sight. Paul met Sophie. He would never forget her name. Her beautiful face and smiling lips. They talked. They laughed. He was falling head-over-heels in love with her amazing personality. These short few minutes left a mark on Paul. It is amazing how the briefest encounters can leave the deepest impressions on us. But all good things must come to an end. Their interaction got caught short in the crowd. An acquaintance called her over to talk with a business contact and Paul and Sophie were parted without exchanging contact info. Paul had fallen madly in love with Sophie, and the only way he knew he could meet her again was the only bit of information he had: she would be at the embassy ball in Florina[1] on Saturday. That came up in their chatting, but nothing else that could assure them of ever crossing paths ever again.

Paul had to get to Florina. The ball was tonight, and the fate of his heart depended on it. But international flights were delayed – and cancelled – as the storm outside raged on. Paul stared out the windows of the airport terminal. The wind blew with heavy gusts, filled with rain from the storm. Torrential downpours coupled with 60 mph winds. This did not bode well. If the flight is cancelled –

"Attention passengers, due to the inclement weather all flights out of Harrisburg International Airport have been cancelled."

What?! No!!

---

[1] Florina is a made-up country in Latin America first introduced in John R. Teevan III, "The Spy's White Dress," *A Mysterious Evening in Vienna* (Albany, NY: Self-published; printed by Create Space Independent Publishing Platform, 2017).

55

Paul desperately waited in line at Delta and American Airlines and United Airlines. Even Air France and British Airways. Even Malaysian Airlines. But none of them would fly him to Florina. "Can I bribe you? Can I pay for all the empty seats in the plane? You name it, I'll pay it. I *must* get to Florina today."

Finally, the agent at the customer service counter for Movrastani Airlines looked left, looked right, then whispered to Paul, "I know a guy …"

Paul smiled.

They met the pilot in the back doorway of the hanger, where all shady deals take place.

"Six thousand dollars."

"What? I'm broke. I can't afford that."

"Then I can't pay for the fuel in my private jet and the risk of flying in the storm – "

"I'm going to an embassy ball. I could get you in if you'd be willing to negotiate the price."

"What type of embassy ball?"

"One with lots of beautiful ladies."

"In that case, this trip is on me, kid. If you can get me into the party, I'll take you there."

And the plane took off through the lightning. Men will do anything for love. Even fly through a storm, and risk it all.

Thunder clamored in the background as explosions of lightning lit up the sky. Which was good because it was night and you couldn't see a thing and the pilot was not instrument-rated –

which means he can't fly in the dark.

Ka-boom! Lightning struck the plane. Both engines failed. The plane went spiraling down.

"Quick, take a parachute!"

"What?!"

"If you don't jump out now, you'll burn to death once we crash. You need to jump. And when you do jump, I recommend you have a parachute on instead of just jumping out of a plane with nothing."

The pilot thrust the parachute into Paul's hands.

"But, but – "

Once the parachute was fully on, Paul hesitated. "Where do I jump?"

"Don't worry, I'll help with that," the pilot said, and he shoved Paul out the door. Both of their parachutes safely deployed with enough time to brace their fall. They slowly came closer to the ground and landed in the courtyard of a beautiful mansion.

"The embassy ball! We're here!" exclaimed Paul.

The men in tuxedos and top hats and waiters with bow ties and ladies in dresses and tiaras stared in disbelief. Someone had just arrived from the sky. Suddenly, the crowd cheered. This was by far the most impressive entrance of any of the guests to the party. Paul and the pilot were heroes.

But where was Sophie? Paul looked around. He searched the entire banquet. But the woman he had fallen in love with was nowhere to be found. Who cares about the ambassador? Paul was here to see Sophie, the love of his life. She would be at this embassy ball tonight, and he would go to the ends of the earth just to meet the woman he had fallen head-over-heels in love with.

"Excuse me, your excellency, where is Señorita González?"

"Oh, she went to the United States. She was flying to Harrisburg to meet some guy she had fallen love with. Why, do you know her?"

# The French Revolution

In Paris, the workers were on strike. The CEO was under scrutiny – and under fire: the protestors were armed. Shots rang out in front of the barricaded door to the CEO's office. Six locks and a steel reinforced door were all that separated the capitalist from the Marxist masses.

"Quick! Call the police!" the CEO desperately shouted to his assistant.

"Mr. CEO, the Ministry of the Interior is under the control of the union."

"Then it's been achieved. Communist revolution." The CEO took a deep breath. "Karl Marx was right. The proletariat wins. What about the Marshall Plan? Containment? The Vietnam War? NATO? The Cold War? All efforts were for naught. It's happened. France has become communist."

The protesters swung a pipe like a battering ram to tear down the door.

"Do you hear that? They're singing the *Internationale*! Traitors!"

"No, Mr. CEO. They're singing the *Marseillaise*."

"It's the same thing."

"Singing your country's national anthem does not make you a traitor. It's patriotic."

The CEO glared at his assistant.

"Our lives are in danger," the CEO moaned, "Once the proletariat takes over – once that door is broken open – the masses will come in and we'll be done for!"

"Not 'us.' 'You' will be. You're in charge of this. I'm just an assistant. They're after the CEO, not his assistant."

"You cocky traitor! When the masses come in here I will feed you to the wolves!"

"I'd never take a bullet for you."

"YOU'RE FIRED!"

"Great. I'm free."

And the assistant opened the door, left, and closed it behind him. The CEO desperately rushed to re-close the locks. And the assistant joined the masses in singing the *Internationale*. But it was patriotic because they sang it in French.

## The DMV

"We can't just give out STD's to people."

"Why not?"

"Are you serious?"

"Jeremy, we're almost out of license plate numbers. Someone's gonna get stuck with the license plate STD 4738 that no one wants. Giving out license plates with the first three letters S-T-D frees up ten thousand new license plate numbers."

"How would *you* like driving a car around with a license plate that says 'STD'?"

"We could give them half off their registration fee."

"So you'd give STD's to poor people?"

The boss walked by and overheard this. Jeremy cringed. Taken out of context, he might get fired from his civil service job. His heart beat went through the roof. Would his boss misinterpret their conversation about giving out STD's to poor people? Was this conversation appropriate for work? Would their boss look at them strangely?

But Allen, the other speaker in their conversation, did not panic. He had worked at the DMV for a while. So he knew.

The boss came into their cubicle.

"You guys are talking about giving out the STD license plates again? It would free up ten thousand much-needed license plate numbers. And we're running out of numbers. Still waiting to hear back from our Commissioner if we can give out offensive license plate numbers. Will let you guys know."

Jeremy was stunned. His boss just supported them giving out STD's.

"Hey, there are lots of people who choose cars that have damaged fenders and broken bumpers. It's unsightly so you save a lot of money. We could give half off the registration fee to anyone willing to get an STD."

"Or we could prank the rich sports car drivers who have so much money and love their fancy cars. We could stick them with an STD license plate on their precious new cars."

"I had a really bad break-up with my girlfriend. Next time she buys a car I'll hit her with an STD license plate."

They both laughed.

And then STD's changed to STI's and their fun was over.

# The Translator

"Ben, have you finished translating the ambassador's speech? The Under Minister of Foreign Affairs wants that speech understandable before his deposition. Why don't you just use an online translator? Why do we pay you? Google Translate is free."

Such is the life of a translator. If the translation is good, the translator is never mentioned. If the translation is bad, the translator is criticized without end. How easy it is to talk but difficult to translate that speech into another language.

Finally, the translators rebelled. They were public employees, so they didn't have the right to strike. So they inserted ridiculous words in the translations that made the politicians who signed the speeches look like idiots.

"Why did the entire Russian delegation laugh during my speech?" asked the Under Minister of Foreign Affairs.

"No idea," replied the translator.

# Harold Stresemann

The coroner turned to the investigator. "That man is dead. I'd say he's been cold for about three hours."

"Is there any evidence of foul play?" asked the investigator.

"Not at all. Clearly natural causes. But what interests me is something I can't figure out yet. Who was he?"

"What do you mean?"

"I've searched all of his pockets. No ID at all."

"Did he have anything in his wallet?"

The coroner manifested a credit card. "The name on the credit card says 'Harold Stresemann.' I called headquarters and they couldn't find any info on this guy. No license. No birthday. Not even a social security number."

"But everyone has a social security number."

"Everyone born in a hospital that the Social Security Administration notices. But what if this man was born at home in the rural parts of our state? He could have slipped through the cracks. You can live a perfectly normal life even if your mom forgot to assign you an SSN at birth."

The coroner's phone rang. "Excuse me, officer, it's the Bureau of Vital Statistics." The coroner took the call. They discussed in detail for a long time. At last, he hung up and turned to the investigator. "There is no record of this man ever being born."

"So how will you write the date of birth when you fill out the death certificate?"

"How will they write the obituary if we don't know anything about this man? We don't even know his age!"

The investigator paused. What would it be like to come into this earth and then leave without leaving a trace? Nobody knew when you came in or when you left, they just knew you existed. How long did you live on this planet? What did you do? What were your accomplishments? Yet sometimes it is liberating to be able to do whatever you want – to live in the moment – and enjoy your time without worrying about what other people will remember about you. You could just be, and enjoy life, without worrying about your legacy.

Suddenly, the dead body moved. He rolled to one side and put his hand over his face. The investigator and coroner were stunned. The man moaned, "Oh, sunburn, I've been tanning for too long. I think I passed out from heat stroke. Can you get me a glass of water?"

The investigator and coroner helped the man as he revived. Finally, they asked the questions. "What's your name?"

"George Lutz."

"Who is Harold Stresemann?"

"Oh, that's just the fake ID and credit card I use to buy beer with while underage."

## The Actress

"I don't want to have sex with that man," the actress said.

"It's just a seven-second make-out scene. Seven seconds and then you're done," explained the director.

"But seven seconds on screen means four days in the studio trying to get the right view with his six-pack and my cleavage. We try again and again to find the balance between something that will get censored and something that will sell. And I don't want to be kissing that creep all day for four days. I – "

"I'll make sure he brushes his teeth and uses breath mints and – "

"No!"

"We get millions more in revenue for this film if there is a passion scene."

"What am I, a hooker? You hired me to be an actress, not a whore. You can't pay me to kiss that bastard. It's not in my contract."

"Ok, I'll call our legal team to find out how we can force you to do what's in the script. This film needs to be shot. And your role is to follow the goddamned script!"

"No means no!"

"If you don't work I can't pay you."

The poor actress. Her boss wants her to kiss someone she doesn't want to. Does she quit her actressing job and spend more time waitressing? Either get hit on by the creepy drunk low-lives at the bar or get pressured into kissing someone she doesn't want to.

But she was also a writer. Nobody knew. Writers are anonymous compared to the public visibility of actresses. And she had connections to all of the screenwriters in Hollywood.

The next day at work she came on set.

"So did you decide to kiss him or resign?" her director asked.

"Didn't you get the new script this morning?"

"What new script?"

Her friend the screenwriter distributed the revised screenplay. The director's jaw dropped.

"There must be some mistake. It says that he's supposed to kiss ... a character played by ... me."

"Yeah. We wanted to make the movie appeal to a wider audience and include more LGBTQ movie-goers. It will sell better if we attract diverse viewers."

"I am not kissing that man!"

"It's in the script. And if you don't follow the script, you get fired."

"What?!"

"It's only seven seconds."

"But seven seconds on screen is four days of making out

with another man!"

"We just need this to sell the film."

"But – "

"Don't worry," the actress reassured, "I'll make sure he brushes his teeth and has a breath mint."

JOHN R. TEEVAN III

# The Flemish Ambassador

*Belgium is made up of two major groups: the French-speaking Walloons and the Dutch-speaking Flemish. Despite the fact that they share a tiny country, the two groups hate each other. When I visited Belgium their country didn't have a government because the Flemish and the Walloons couldn't agree on a leader. It had been over a year and they still didn't have a Prime Minister. Which is ironic because the European Commission, the powerful executive branch of the EU, is headquartered in Brussels. But the local politicians could not decide on a leader for Belgium. Historians describe Belgium like an old married couple: they've been together for so many years that they hate each other but don't split up.*

*The following story is what would happen if they did go separate ways – and Wallonia joined France and Flanders joined the Netherlands. It would be the divorce of the century.*

The Austrian ambassador met with the Flemish ambassador. Wait – Flemish ambassador? Is Flanders an independent nation? Yes and no. That question is the big, politically-charged question everyone is asking. Belgium had split in two. After years of fighting, the two groups decided to go their separate ways. The Walloons were petitioning to become a département of France, and the Flemish were lobbying to join the Netherlands. Brussels was divided between the two opposing forces – just like East and West Berlin. The fate of the capital was not yet decided because, after all, the schism – the fall of Belgium – was not officially recognized yet. The

Flemish ambassador was meeting with each foreign minister in Europe one-by-one.

The Austrian ambassador sat down with his Flemish counterpart. The question of recognizing Flemish sovereignty was a touchy issue that must be handled diplomatically. Rather than articulate his country's position, the Austrian ambassador did what diplomatic geniuses do. He replied to the question about Flemish independence with another question instead of an answer.

"What is the position of the European Commission?" asked the Austrian ambassador.

"Well, considering that their headquarters is in Brussels, I'd say they're on the fence. After the split is formalized, Brussels could go either French or Dutch. Without knowing what will happen, the European Commission has been silent. They don't want to offend the country that will soon own their city."

"So what are you asking for from the Austrians?"

"Diplomatic recognition."

"France will kill me!" the Austrian ambassador exclaimed.

"But if you're not diplomatically recognizing the Flemish delegation, why are you making a state visit to the ambassador of the newly-independent Flemish nation?"

"We're just friends getting together for coffee. Nothing official."

"But we're in the grand state room of the Flemish royal court."

The Austrian ambassador thought to himself, "Damn! I just made a big diplomatic mistake." Whether the Flemish ambassador intended it or not, inviting the Austrian over for coffee was a trap in him making a state visit to diplomatically recognize Flemish independence.

"Um, I'm out of cream in my coffee. Would you like to get a cup at a coffee shop – um, far away from here – maybe at a Starbucks in Switzerland – somewhere that's out of the way so no reporters can find us?"

"Would you like to come to my living room?"

"Is it the official residence of the Flemish ambassador?"

"Um, yes."

"Let's just get some chocolates and waffles downtown."

And they enjoyed some Belgian waffles and chocolates while sitting next to the Manneken Pis fountain and discussing diplomatic secrets in the public square. Being diplomats, they were both fluent in so many languages that they easily switched to Tahitian so none of the passerby understood their conversations. But what about the paparazzi? Well, diplomats are often forgotten. Soldiers are heroes. Actors are celebrities. But the multilingual geniuses that leave their families and go to dangerous far-away lands and put their lives at risk for their nation – the civil servants that keep our world running – are so unrecognized that nobody recognized their own ambassador. So nobody paid any mind to the two men eating waffles at the fountain and the diplomats continued their negotiations undisturbed. No paparazzi. No reporters slamming Austria for intervening in Belgium. Just two guys eating waffles near a fountain.

The Flemish ambassador mustered enough courage to broach the awkward question, "So, where are we going? Are we in a relationship? Or are our countries just friends? Was this a date –

an official diplomatic interaction of two nations getting to know each other? Or is it just two friends getting coffee? Or is it something more? What is our relationship? Will Austria set up an embassy in Flanders? What is the nature of our interaction today?"

The Austrian ambassador replied, "We just met for coffee."

"Yes, we had an official state visit by the ambassador of Austria who was received by the Flemish ambassador."

"We just met for coffee."

"So we're just friends? Nothing more?"

"We just met for coffee."

"So we met. The Austrian ambassador met with the Flemish ambassador thereby recognizing Flanders. We did meet, didn't we?"

The Austrian ambassador paused. He was caught in a trap. A catch-22. Saying they didn't meet would be perjury. Yet saying they did meet would be a diplomatic bombshell, obligating Austria to take a side and get sucked into the conflict between Flanders and Wallonia – and by extension France and the Netherlands. What would the Austrian ambassador say? How would he reply without making a faux pas? The Austrian ambassador paused, reflected and then remembered the wise old saying about diplomacy:

> "If a diplomat says 'yes' it means 'perhaps.'
> If a diplomat says 'perhaps' it means 'no.'
> If a diplomat says 'no' he is not a diplomat.
> If a lady says 'no' it means 'perhaps.'
> If a lady says 'perhaps' it means 'yes.'

If a lady says 'yes' she is not a lady."[2]

The Austrian ambassador looked up at the Flemish ambassador and replied, "Austria is a democracy, and as such these matters are a decision of The People. The issue of recognizing Flemish independence will be submitted to Parliament. I will send a cable to my Minister of Foreign Affairs right away so we can have an answer for you."

"But that could take six years for Parliament to crank their wheels before the bill makes it to the floor so they can debate the issue before making a decision," the Flemish ambassador complained.

"I know. And they probably won't even make a decision. They'll submit it to The People through a referendum, that way the politicians can wash their hands and not get blamed for the fallout either way the people decide."

"All this bureaucratic nonsense just so you can answer the simple 'yes' or 'no' question of whether or not we met when we met?"

"Yup."

"Damn. I was looking for our countries to hook up, but I guess I'll have to find a different country that can give me a straight answer of whether or not we're in a relationship."

"Hmm. Well, who do you have to choose from? The Americans have avoided entangling alliances since their very first president, so you won't have very much luck with the U.S. But, after

---

[2] My translation of Voltaire. There is also an adapted version by Talleyrand. Note that both of the contributors to this hilarious, eloquent saying are French. French is the traditional language of diplomacy, and also the language of love – both of which are touched on by this quote.

all, their only ally was France, and France is your enemy because Wallonia is joining France. Hmm, you'd better marry into one of the royal families in Europe. That's the best way to formalize a political alliance because you're in the same family as that nation's king."

The Flemish ambassador paused. "So I have to go on an online dating app and post that I only want to date women who are princesses of royal blood and next in line to the throne? Nobody will write back."

"Actually, I'm sure you'll get lots of scammers and con artists."

The Flemish ambassador sighed. How would he ever get an alliance?

Then, suddenly a bomb exploded a few feet away from them. A tank crushed through Manneken Pis. The German air force flew overhead. World War One was beginning. Suddenly both Flanders and Wallonia were inundated with invitations for an alliance from Italy, England, Russia, Spain, and of course both France and Germany. Flanders and Wallonia were delighted to have so many offers for alliances and diplomatic recognition and military backing. What the Flemish ambassador called "friendship with benefits." And then suddenly both Flanders and Wallonia were overrun completely by the German military for the rest of the war. But what about Belgium? What about Flanders? What about Wallonia? What about the nation? The people of Belgium waited. And waited. And waited. And waited for the fighting to end so they could see what the post-war order would look like.

## The Church Discovers that God is a Woman

The monk was a biblical scholar – a world expert. He devoted his entire life to studying the scriptures. He took vows of poverty and chastity to devote his entire life to God. The monk taught at four local colleges, and people flocked to his lectures on Christian doctrine. One day, while deep in thought contemplating the Torah, the monk unearthed a life-changing discovery. God was a woman! He immediately phoned the archbishop.

"Archbishop O'Brien, I just made a discovery that alters Christianity! God is female!"

"But how do you know?"

"It says so in the original Bible."

"But that's written in Latin. Latin is a dead language. Nobody speaks it."

"I spent three years studying Latin so I could translate this."

"But the Latin is only a translation of Hebrew. How do you know what the original said if you're just reading the translation?"

"I spent two years in Israel to become fluent in Hebrew so I could translate this."

"Are you sure the Bible says that?"

"Yes. Let me cite the verse. It says so in the book of – "

"I believe you. Let me check with the Church's official scholar. I'll call you back."

The archbishop called the Church's in-house scholar. "Hey, a researcher just discovered that God is female."

"Yeah, God was originally written as female. But back then the feminist movement was just beginning. Women were starting to ask for rights. To protect tradition and delay the Women's Liberation Movement, the church elders decided to write the Torah using the masculine pronoun for God, not the feminine pronoun."

The archbishop's jaw dropped. "But if this secret gets out, it could destroy society's faith in religion as we know it! Synagogues, mosques, protestant churches, Catholic cathedrals – our credibility would be shattered! This cover-up was meant to protect tradition and religion. But once the word gets out it will destroy the very things it was meant to protect! Wait until the religious scholars find out. They will criticize – "

"The religious scholars already know," said the Church's in-house scholar. "They considered changing God to 'She.' But then they'd have to rewrite every book of the Bible. And that's a lot of work, considering nobody speaks Ancient Greek or Aramaic anymore. So they just left it the way it was. And Bibles keep getting printed with 'He' instead of 'She.'"

"But the Bible is wrong, then."

"Archbishop, the people will believe anything you tell them, whether you're wrong or right. If you say this book is Holy, people will buy it, even if it's written wrong."

"But the publishers are printing lies!"

"Archbishop," the Church's in-house scholar warned, "If

you disclose the truth and put those companies out of business – if people stop buying Bibles – we will be out of work and unemployed. If people stop believing what the Bible says, then nobody will come to Church."

"And I need those dollar bills in the offering basket because they pay my salary," the archbishop sighed.

"So we'll keep the fact that God is a woman – we'll keep that as a secret between you and me?"

The archbishop agreed.

"But the monk who discovered it. He knows."

"Promote him to cardinal. Keep him away from the universities he teaches at. The honor – and the money – of being a cardinal should shut him up."

"Brilliant."

And the word never got out that God was a woman. The Women's Liberation Movement was slowed but not stopped. Men held onto their power for thousands and thousands of years until finally women won the right to vote. But women have no reproductive rights or divorce rights within the jurisdiction of the Catholic Church. Things would be different if everyone knew that God was female. But the authority for the scriptures remains in the hands of the Church, far away from the feminists and others who might discover the true gender of God. And that is why the Church does not allow women to become priests.

JOHN R. TEEVAN III

# The Maginot Line is Breached

"Idiots!" French General Weygand shouted as he tore down the map from the wall, "Not one of you thought about what would happen if the Germans went *around* the Maginot Line?"

"Monsieur le général, crossing neutral Belgium – we – we knew that was a possibility – "

"Imbeciles! The Germans did this to us in World War One! Have you learned *nothing* from the lessons of history?!"

"Monsieur le général, we were constructing a wall. But it would be insulting if we built it along the French border behind the Belgians. That would tell our ally, 'We're so sure that you're going to get your asses kicked that we're going to build this behind you to protect ourselves when you get conquered.' Belgium is our ally, and that would be a diplomatic slap in the face."

Weygand, in a fit of rage, gave his lieutenant a slap in the face. "*That* is a slap in the face! And as for Belgium: What good is it to have allies if they are useless? Belgium has already surrendered to Hitler. In a few hours Paris will capitulate. Unless we can find a solution. This is all your fault! You idiots built a massive, expensive defensive fortification at taxpayer expense and the Germans just went around it!"

"It would have been a slap in the face to Belgium if we – "

Whack! "*That*, my friend, is a slap in the face!" said the general as he slapped the major. "And you deserve less than the Belgians. They lost because you incompetently didn't finish your wall all the way to the Atlantic. The Belgians deserved better. Their blood is on your hands."

The lieutenant whispered to the major, "Well, on the bright side, Weygand will go down in history as a failure. He bears the title of commander-in-chief of France's defenses. Meanwhile, history will never know our names. We can fail left and right and will never get the blame in history. Meanwhile, Weygand will forever be remembered as a loser in the history books."

*Note that in this story the lieutenant and the major do not have names. The behind-the-scenes leaders in history are always forgotten – for better or for worse. I am sure they are delighted to be anonymous. Poor General Weygand.*

"Democracy will die! The Third Republic ceases to exist," moaned Weygand, "Parliament resigns. It all falls on Philippe Pétain."

*Well, as least Weygand isn't the only one who gets blamed. Now another figurehead will live in infamy. Let us see how Marshall Philippe Pétain and Pierre Laval are constructing the new order in Vichy.*

"Pierre, should we collaborate with the Germans?" asked Pétain.

"Oui, oui, monsieur le maréchal! Wheeling and dealing gives us the best possible advantages in negotiations," replied Laval.

"Isn't there a risk collaborating with the Nazis?"

Laval thought to himself, "Yes, of course. Hitler is a bloodthirsty bastard. But if I sign a treaty with him, he'll treat me better. And then when shit goes down, history will remember that you were in charge, not me. You're the World War One hero that everyone loves – and soon everyone will hate. But I'll wash the blood off my hands. Because I'm the behind-the-scenes leader. And you're the figurehead. Every Frenchman has a copy of your portrait in their living room – not mine. And soon they'll be burning you in effigy – not me."

"I'm sorry, Pierre, I didn't hear what you said, you look like you're in a day dream," said Pétain to Laval who was scheming all kinds of dark, bloody behind-the-scenes back-stabbing plots. But on the outside he appeared to be innocently daydreaming. "I'm sorry, I didn't hear what you said. Do you think there is a risk to collaborating with the Nazis?"

Laval scratched his eyebrow. "Monsieur le maréchal, there is a risk to everything. We never know what will happen until we try. Negotiating will give us the best possible treatment when Germany conquers Europe. Will the Nazis oppress our citizens? Only history will know. Will they treat us better if we collaborate? Probably."

"But the blood will be on our hands," worried Pétain.

Laval thought to himself, "No, Pétain, the blood will be on *your* hands. Not mine." But instead, he replied, "Look, we lost the war. There will be bloodshed in whatever we choose. A little bloodshed on your hands could save thousands of French lives."

"But, Pierre, the Jews. French Jews might be oppressed by Hitler."

"Monsieur le maréchal, look at Captain Dreyfus. You can't say that Jews aren't already oppressed by France."

Pétain scratched his head. "Well, here goes nothing." He signed the surrender in the same train car that the Germans signed the Armistice in World War One. War was avoided and peace was preserved. The economy prospered as Germany and France combined. Every household in France had a portrait of Pétain – their hero. « Vive le maréchal ! » the masses shouted as the popular Marshall paraded. He was their savior who spared them from Nazi conquest.

"I wonder how long Pétain will remain popular?" asked his Under Minister.

"Wait 'til the allies start to win in the Liberation of France, the Nazis take over unoccupied Southern France and the Holocaust is revealed. I'd give it two years," replied Laval.

"And until then?"

"Until then, Charles de Gaulle is a deranged deserter, Jean Moulin and his French Resistance are terrorists, and Pétain is our national hero."

"Travail, Famille, Patrie."

"Vive la France."

# A Note on The Maginot Line is Breached

*"Travail, Famille, Patrie" [work, family, country] was Pétain's slogan and the rally cry of Vichy's French State. "Vive la France" were Laval's last words as he was executed for treason after the allies liberated France. They are also the last words of this piece.*

*Laval collaborated with the Nazis – actively sending French Jews off to concentration camps in Eastern Europe to be massacred. Yet he claims that in return his collaboration protected his nation from harsher treatment by the occupying Germans. Whether you believe his story or not, justice was served: Laval was executed by firing squad after the Nazi regime crumbled. Pétain, the head of the French State, was pardoned because of his World War One heroism. He was old and wouldn't have lived much longer anyway, so an execution was seen as not necessary. Still, would you rather die quickly and painlessly while shouting "Vive la France!" as bullets race over your head, or would you rather spend the rest of your life with shame and guilt and blood on your hands? Who got the worse punishment: Laval or Pétain?*

JOHN R. TEEVAN III

## Atomic Romance

"Chloe, hurry! It's gonna be too late!"

Chloe scratched her head. Doing quantum physics under pressure never ends well.

"How much Uranium should I inject?" Julian pressed.

Chloe crumbled under pressure. She was never good at math. But now if the universe depended on it...

"The U-235 is getting unstable! If we don't disable this bomb, all of Miami will go ka-boom!"

The complexities of the 21$^{st}$ Century. Disabling a bomb means disabling an atomic bomb. And the bomb technicians now need to know nuclear physics.

The Japanese always held a grudge against the Americans for Hiroshima. But now this atomic bomb that fell astray in downtown Miami during a test offshore. This was karma coming back to America – and revenge for having invented the atomic bomb.

"Julian, I think this is it. Our lives are over. We'll never see our families again. Your face will be the last I ever see. This bomb can't be disabled. There's no sense in running: we'll only die from radiation poisoning. So let's stay here and we'll die together. A quick and painless end is the best we can hope for."

"Chloe, I love you."

"What?"

"I've always had a crush on you, but now it seems we'll breathe our last. And I can't leave this world without telling you that."

Chloe was stunned. "I – I – I was going to give a confession, too. I stole your donut from the break room. It's not quite as deep as yours, but I don't want to leave the earth with that on my conscience either."

"Chloe, your face is the last face I will ever see. Soon my life will be complete. But I would rather die with you in my eyes than with anyone else. So what do you say? Do you love me?"

"I, I – I – "

Suddenly, Julian's cell phone rang. The goofy ringtone interrupted the solemn occasion.

"Should I even pick up?" he wondered, "What will answering this phone call do to improve the quality of my last few moments on earth?"

"It could be the bomb squad bunker," Chloe burst out and picked up Julian's cell phone.

"Hello. You have been selected to take a brief survey – "

Chloe hung up the phone. By her calculations, they had between 45 and 60 seconds before the uranium becomes unstable and their lives go ka-boom.

What would you do if you only had 45 seconds to live? Certainly not waste time on telemarketers. What would be most meaningful to fill your remaining time? Some will fill the entire 45 seconds worrying and trying to think of how to use it without actually using it. What would you choose to do as your last action on this earth? With limited time, your time becomes more valuable.

Julian gazed at Chloe's beautiful eyes and smiled. If she was the last face he would ever see, at least he would die happy. And Chloe reminisced about the delicious donut she had savored yesterday from Julian's lunch box in the break room. Their time was up. Ka-boom.

# The Commissioner of Elections

The Commissioner of Elections sat back on the couch and turned on the TV. Democracy is not a spectator sport. But tonight the results were going to be on TV and he couldn't wait to watch. Even the most powerful actors become spectators to their own actions.

For the ninth Congressional district, the race was tight. Absentee ballots were being opened.

"No! No! Please, no!"

The election results were within two percent. State election law requires manual recount. The results were too close to call, and they had to be fair.

"Noooooooooo!"

The Commissioner of Elections had been up since 4 o'clock in the morning, monitoring polls and investigating fraud allegations. Does it really matter for one vote whether Mr. Penington voted and then voted again, signing in for Mr. Cabot? One little vote and all of the masses of election fraud paperwork for investigating one tiny vote. In the scheme of things, will one vote really matter? The Election Commissioner was tired. He had been monitoring polls from opening at 5am to closing at 9pm. It's almost like all year he prepares for this one day. This very long day. Like Santa Claus. And then he's done and can relax until next November. But no. This recount. The Election Commissioner put on his coat and drove to the Board of Elections downtown.

The Deputy Commissioners approached him. There were

53,000 ballots to count. One by one.

"We gave it to the Democrats last time. Let's give it to the Republicans this time. It's only fair."

"It's less than 2% difference. The People won't care either way it goes. They're happy with both candidates. The votes are half and half. We can save time and, instead of counting each ballot, just flip a coin. The People won't mind – they're split 50-50. Nobody will notice either way we declare the election."

The Election Commissioner took out a quarter. "May the better candidate win."

The results were announced. And the Board of Elections went home and got some much-needed sleep. Democracy is not a spectator sport. Sometimes the man who flips the coin decides it all.

# Life Insurance

"So why are you interested in this position?"

"The life insurance."

"You mean – "

"I'm 97 years old. I'm gonna die any day. You can't buy a life insurance policy at my age – it's too expensive. But all of your employees are covered. If I am on the payroll, then my grandkids will get $10,000 when I croak."

"So you're working here so you can die?"

"But I won't say you worked me to death."

"Don't you need the paycheck? Did you live too long and not have enough savings to sustain your retirement?"

"No. I don't need the money. As soon as you hire me I'm going on vacation leave. I've got cruises paid out for the next six months. I don't need the money. I just want to be on the payroll. As a gift to my grandkids."

"Well, did you submit an application for the position?"

"Yes, it's right here." The old man rummaged through his briefcase to find the papers.

"No, I mean, you need to apply online."

"Oh, well, in that case, the $10,000 isn't worth it. You can keep your ten grand. I will never learn how to use a computer. Goodbye."

## The Decision that Changed the World

"Prime Minister! General Weygand just called. The front has been breached! Paris – our entire nation – is in grave danger! The Germans have crossed the Ardennes. Unforeseeable. Impossible. But this is our present reality. A terrifying reality – a nightmare. We must evacuate the capital at once!" Terror was evident in the colonel's voice. "The British and French forces are evacuating at Dunkirk. It's a disaster – a fiasco. Disorder reigns. Prime Minister, it is imperative that you – " and then: boom. Then: static. The colonel was no more.

What would it be like to be French Prime Minister Paul Reynaud? To get that phone call and have moments to decide the fate of your nation? The second-largest empire in the world – with an army that had the reputation of being the strongest army in the world – was toppled. The news shocked the world. What the Germans could not achieve in four years in World War One Hitler accomplished in four weeks in World War Two. France was conquered.

These are the moments that define our personality. Our personal courage and our moral fiber. As Thomas Paine wrote, "These are the times that try men's souls."[3]

Reynaud had two choices: surrender and collaborate so the Germans will treat the French better once they occupy all of Europe. Work together to build a united Europe. Or flee to Morocco and fight

---

[3] Thomas Paine, "The American Crisis," *The American Crisis*, (1776), University of Groningen, http://www.let.rug.nl/usa/documents/1776-1785/thomas-paine-american-crisis/chapter-i---the-american-crisis---december-23-1776.php.

to the last man. Many more Frenchmen will die in an endlessly destructive war that they could lose anyway.

But why do we fight? Our ideology. Our rhetoric. Léon Blum articulated his new administration's goal in occupying the government with the power of the people to prevent it from falling into the control of the fascists.[4] Woodrow Wilson, when shaping the American ideology for World War One, proclaimed: "The world must be safe for democracy."[5] But where is France's *esprit du corps* going into World War Two? A war without an ideology will always lose. So where does Reynaud's moral compass point? What will he decide?

*The original text of this piece was written in alternating French and English. It is this duality – this dichotomy of two languages – as if struggling to make a decision between two choices. To fight or to surrender? What will the French Prime Minister decide? The back-and-forth disagreeing between French and English languages in this piece also represents conflicts between London and Paris over continuing to fight or surrendering to the Nazis as these two allies went in different directions. Yet this moment of crisis and disagreement and words lost in translation is best expressed in my stream-of-consciousness alternating between French and English writing. However, I have translated it all to English here to facilitate access to all readers.*

---

[4] Jacques Delperrié de Bayac, *Histoire du Front Populaire* (Paris: Fayard, 1972), p. 133.

[5] Woodrow Wilson, "The Challenge Accepted: President Wilson's Address to Congress, April 2, 1917," (speech, Washington, DC, April 2, 1917), British Library, https://www.bl.uk/collection-items/president-woodrow-wilsons-address-to-congress-2-april-1917.

So what does Reynaud do in time of crisis? Prime Minister Reynaud fires his Vice Prime Minister, replacing him with old, tired, retired war hero Philippe Pétain. Then the Prime Minister resigns. Parliament dissolves, passing laws suspending their constitution – an act that historians call a suicide – and entrusting Pétain with creating a new constitution that never comes to fruition. Pierre Laval actively collaborates with the Nazis, deporting French Jews to concentration camps. And the Holocaust and resulting horrors are history.

But what would have happened if Reynaud chose to fight?

He could have changed history. He could be a hero. He could have prevented the Holocaust. He could have saved millions of lives – on both sides – all over the world. Instead of voluntarily handing over the French navy to the services of the occupying Germans, the forces could have been used to defend against Nazi expansion. Instead of French POWs being sent to forced labor camps in Germany to build weapons for the Nazis, these soldiers would defend France – and fight for liberty, equality, fraternity: the motto of the French Republic.

Here is an account of what would have happened if Reynaud had decided to fight:

Paris was burned. The Louvre, the National Assembly, the Eiffel Tower – destroyed by hate. After having occupied Paris, Hitler burnt it to the ground to show his power and spread fear among the French, who were fighting from Morocco.

"It is now or never!" FDR proclaimed to the isolationist Congress. "If we don't act now, France, our ally, will fall. Europe will be conquered by fear."

Senate Republicans, wanting to avoid foreign entanglements in another European war, filibustered to prevent a declaration of war. And America remained isolationist.

But FDR still managed to negotiate a lend-lease agreement with de Gaulle just as he had done with Churchill. The French provisional government elected Charles de Gaulle as Prime Minister. Pétain, 84 years old, retired to play boules and smoke cigarettes while keeping his World War One hero reputation relatively untarnished.

Indochina organized a draft to fight the Nazis on behalf of their French colonial leaders. After World War Two, the French nation was grateful to their Vietnamese brothers-in-arms. Ho Chi Minh went on a golfing retreat with President de Gaulle, and the two amicably negotiated independence. De Gaulle, grateful for the Vietnamese troops he commanded that saved France, graciously gave autonomy to Vietnam, Laos and Cambodia. There was no Vietnam War. No Vietnam Memorial in Washington, DC. No traumatic, turbulent anti-war hippie protests in the '60s. Instead of protesting the government and the draft, Americans in the 1960s worked with LBJ to accomplish The Great Society. Poverty was eliminated, and health and education flourished. It's amazing what money can do when it's not used to fight a Vietnam War.

Because France was still a world superpower – and hadn't lost its control in a World War Two defeat – when George W. Bush wanted to invade Iraq and Jacques Chirac vetoed UN support, the U.S. did not invade Iraq. Freedom fries were not a phenomenon – you can't offend a world superpower. And the Iraq War quagmire – seventeen years and counting – never occurred.

The world looked to Paul Reynaud – who changed the world – as a hero. Or as a coward. Depending upon his one decision.

## The Life of a Superstar

"Gabe, could you get my pen?"

Gabe looked at the writing desk in the studio. There were fifty-some-odd pens scattered all over the desk. Some with beautiful ink for autographing paperbacks at book signings. Some with comfortable gripping to write – profusely – pages and pages without end. You need to be comfortable when expressing ideas – for hours. Some pencils to draw – capable of being magically erased to create a perfect image – a representation without mistakes – identical to reality. There were pens with blue ink, red ink, green ink – to edit the writing and make annotations in different colors while revising.

"Olivia, could you specify which pen?"

"The one I use when I write in Spanish."

"Ok. Gotcha." Gabe knew immediately which pen she wanted. When one is close with a writer one knows which pen she uses to write in Spanish. Even when there are fifty other pens on the desk to choose from.

"Thanks, dear. I'll be at the café." She kissed Gabe.

"Should I wait for you for lunch? Or start without you?"

"Don't wait for me for dinner. I don't know what time I'll be back, but don't hold your breath."

Gabe looked up at the chandelier, the fifteen-bedroom home – more like mansion – and the rich royalty checks that payed for it all. When inspiration strikes, one must capture the ideas. No books means no royalties. No royalties means Olivia and Gabe are nothing more than starving artists. The only difference between a starving artist and a superstar is that the superstar always carries a pen in her pocket to capture ideas when inspiration strikes. The starving artist has written nothing – the moments of inspiration escape her because she didn't have a pen in her pocket – and thus has published nothing and has no checks from her publishers to buy food. Collapsed of hunger, she is starved of food, but more importantly her soul is starved of ideas – inspiration escapes her. The lack of food can deprive the body of its vitality, but the lack of creativity – the lack of ideas – the lack of inspiration that feeds our soul – can deprive the soul of life.

Olivia went to the café. With her pen that she uses when she writes in Spanish. She wrote – furiously – nonstop – with all the passion of a mind lit up with inspiration. She wrote an entire novel that day – and night – and following morning.

After having written an entire novel, she packed up her papers and left. She gave a huge tip to the café – as always. It is thanks to them that she has a place to write. Ambiance is essential for her creativity, and she is always grateful – and generous – with her favorite café. The subway had closed. It was 3 o'clock in the morning. She hailed a cab.

"Good evening, ma'am. Where are you going?" asked the driver.

Instead of saying her address, she said, "I'm Olivia. You might know where my mansion is. It's near – "

The driver looked in his rear view mirror. It was her!! The famous writer!! In his car!! He couldn't believe his eyes.

"Miss Beauvais! Oh, what an honor to have you in my car! Yes, with pleasure I will take you home. Everyone knows your famous mansion. You don't need to tell me the address. I know how to get there."

They talked together during the ride. Then, they were at the gate of her mansion. She got out.

"That'll be 19 euros" said the driver.

She gave him a € 50 note.

"Oh, sure, I can make change for a 50."

"No, it's a tip. You can keep the change," she replied.

"What?"

"You didn't take pictures of me when I was in your taxi. So I'm thanking you."

"Taxi drivers took pictures of you without your permission?!" he asked.

"Yup. Even while driving."

"But – ?!"

"I'm famous. All men want me. For many taxi drivers meeting me is their claim to fame. They are documenting our encounter by taking photos and – as soon as our trip is finished – posting the pictures on Instagram for bragging rights."

"What a curse! You are intelligent. You are beautiful. You are creative. You are rich. You make great conversation. Any man's heart would fall for you. You've written more books than the entire collection our public library owns. You have all the talent in the world. But your success has ruined you."

"I'm a celebrity. And that's the price I pay."

The driver, Steven, looked at Olivia. He felt pity for Olivia, but his passions were soon enthralled with a mixture of feelings toward Olivia, who was about to leave. Admiration for the city's most famous, accomplished author. Lustful desire towards this hot celebrity who was right next to him yet yearning to be even closer to her beautiful body. Incredulously not believing that he just met this famous superstar. Despair that this interaction would soon be over and they would never meet again. How he wished this moment would never end.

Steven said, "In case you ever need a taxi to take you home after writing at the café again, Miss Beauvais – "

"Call me Olivia."

"Miss Olivia, in case you ever need a taxi, here is my number." He gave her his card.

"And here's mine," she said, writing on a Post-it Note her personal cell phone number. "Call me."

Steven could not believe his eyes. It was a dream.

"Miss Olivia, can I ask you – "

"Olivia."[6]

"Olivia, can I ask you a favor?"

---

[6] This story was originally written in French. In the original French version, Olivia asks Steven to use "tu," the familiar form of address for close friends, instead of "vous," the formal way of addressing someone with more distance. "Tu" and "vous" both mean "you." Rather than translate her utterance "tu" as "you" and lose the semantic distinction of the "tu"/"vous" register being communicated, I translated the English version for Steven saying "vous" as "Miss Olivia" and then she corrects him by telling him to call her "Olivia" where the "tu" would have been. The way it is expressed in French is much richer and more deep in terms of communicating their relationship becoming closer.

Her seductive gaze peered deep into the depths of Steven's eyes. Her body language seemed to say, "Yes, I will do anything you want with you tonight." But her silence spoke more than any words could express.

He asked, "Could you sign your autograph on a piece of paper for me?"

"With pleasure," she said seductively, "I have copies of my new book inside. I could autograph one – and for you I won't charge. Would you like to come inside?"

Steven's heart raced. His body melted. His blood pumped faster than he had ever felt. There was only one response. "Yes." Steven followed Olivia into her home.

But what about Gabe, Olivia's lover? Where was he? It's complicated. He was Olivia's partner. What an honor. What a pleasure. What a burden.

With all the pleasures that come with this sought-after role comes also dealing with her many infidelities. After all, she is the superstar, not him. She is the billionaire, not him. Gabe – what is his role? Is he her lover? Her butler? Her fiancé? Her assistant?

He's there to help Olivia with her professional writing business – Gabe is an accountant and takes care of the book sales and marketing. He's there as her lover – when Olivia's amorous desires are not with someone else. But the famous celebrity has a passion that is never satisfied. The same passion and energy that inspire her creative writing. The same passion that makes Olivia cheat on Gabe all the time.

What goes on inside Gabe's head? What are the deepest thoughts and emotions he toils with? What is he really feeling on the inside?

JOHN R. TEEVAN III

Actually, he couldn't care less about her cheating. He has a mansion that he didn't have to pay for. He has the joy of living with Olivia. She is the most-desired lady in the entire city, and he has the honor of being her significant other. She cheats on him, yes, but at least he gets to be with her more than any of the other men do.

It's not your usual relationship. Gabe's Facebook account says, "In a relationship" while Olivia's says "Single." After a few months, he changed it to "It's complicated." And that's how it is. After all, they're not married, so her marital status for legal documents is "Single." But that doesn't mean she isn't in a relationship with Gabe. When she chooses to be. On her terms. When she's not spending the night with someone else.

Steven asked how Olivia lived in a relationship with so many infidelities.

"I'm an artist. I value independence. I like my freedom. If I had to go on tour with a wedding ring and a baby in a stroller, I wouldn't get the same experience as I would traveling alone. The adventure of exploring – going to every city and seeing the world as a celebrity – it wouldn't be worth going on tour if I had a ring. I fall in love with all my fans. I satisfy every one of my desires. If Gabe didn't allow my freedom in our relationship then going on tour wouldn't be worth it. At least it wouldn't be the same sense of adventure. I'm a bestselling author: I have the life of a rock star and the brains of a professor. Men fall head-over-heels for me."

"So what's it like when you're on tour? You give book talks, see the tourist attractions, go to Meetups, write, get inspired for new stories from your travels. But do you really meet men?"

"I have a lover in every city."

Steven's heart began to race out of excitement.

"And tonight," she said, "you're the lucky man." She started unbuttoning Steven's shirt, revealing his muscular chest. "What do you say?" she asked.

*I was going to write Steven's reaction, but then realized: there really only is one possible response. A superstar just gave him an offer he will never forget. Rather than write, "He said, 'Yes,'" I leave the ending to your wildest imagination.*

JOHN R. TEEVAN III

# The Freed Spirit

The worst crime the man ever committed was becoming complacent in losing his freedom. He was arrested and locked in jail. He spent six years behind bars. The judge found him guilty of the crime he never committed. Finally, after six years in his cell with mice and nothing to eat but goulash, he lost hope.

Pain is unbearable, but suffering has no bounds.

The man gazed out the window. But it wasn't a window. It was just a hole in the wall of his cell.

Was he a man? Or a criminal? The law labeled him as a criminal. And the guards treated him accordingly.

Who held the key to his freedom?

But, alas.

Suffering is only our reaction to the pain that life presents us.

And more important than freedom from his cell was the freedom of his spirit. The law kept his body locked up, but his mind kept his spirit locked up.

Write! He must write his thoughts. Mental reflection freed his spirit.

All of a sudden, he realized that he was in prison in his own mind. And he controlled his own thoughts.

His cell didn't have a window. It had a hole in the wall. A

hole that was big enough for him to fit through and escape.

And he decided to leave his cell. He left prison. And he became a man again. He was no longer a criminal. He had freed his soul.

## The Office of Personnel Management

The Office of Personnel Management is the HR authority for the federal government. When there's a toxic office or incompetent employees or abusive bosses, they receive complaints and come up with solutions to workplace problems. Every day they receive complaints from employees. Too much office politics in the EPA, lazy government workers in the IRS, pay disparity in the CDC between the doctors and the rest of the employees. But one day the HR specialist monitoring the general HR email inbox got one that caught his eye. He printed the email and then burst into the Director's office, bypassing six layers of secretaries and assistants to the Assistant to the Director and the Assistant to the Director until he reached the Director.

"Jesse, what is it?"

"I have something for you," he said as he gave the email to the Director.

"Jesse, you know those go through our coordinators in the department of – "

"No, Mr. Director, this one you need to see."

"But – "

"It's a toxic workplace complaint. Office: The Oval Office."

The Director of the Office of Personnel Management rushed out from his desk to see the paper and read the complaint thoroughly. The Secretary of Education was alleging that the Secretary of Energy was creating a toxic workplace through backstabbing office politics. The President's Chief of Staff was doing nothing, since he had already taken a side, and the President was off with the Secretary of State on a world tour at taxpayer expense. The complaint – written anonymously to protect that Secretary's job – said the pay disparity was tearing the cabinet apart – since all federal employees' salaries are posted online as public information. The Secretary of Veterans' Affairs was a disabled veteran who was always late to cabinet meetings because he was so old and so slow and it took forever for the Secret Service to search his wheelchair that never fit through the White House metal detector. The Secretary of Health and Human Services always complained about how much work she had to do since her department was charged with implementing ObamaCare – and how little work the Administrator of the EPA had to do. A conservative administration was elected, so the Environmental Protection Agency decided to stop protecting the environment. Which meant that the Administrator and his EPA now did absolutely nothing. Unless, of course, you count playing solitaire during work time as doing something. The Secretary of Defense was competing for funding that the Secretary of State wanted. And the President had to decide between peace or war – spending money on diplomacy or bombs. The Department of State and the Department of Defense should be working together to enact policy. But the cabinet room was as dysfunctional as a train wreck.

The Director of the Office of Personnel Management sighed. The President of the United States – the most powerful man in the world – his fate was in this bureaucrat's hands. If this email got out, scandal would make headlines. The President's re-election campaign this November would be shattered. The Democrats would retake the White House – and maybe Congress too. What would the Director do?

The Director was a Republican. And as a federal employee, he was a politician skilled in diplomacy. "Jesse, reply to the complaint email: 'Matters in the Oval Office fall under the jurisdiction of the President who makes decisions on these matters. The Office of Personnel Management defers to him.' Send that today. And Jesse, please delete that email. And never – *ever* – speak of this again."

JOHN R. TEEVAN III

## The Pharmaceutical Salesman

The pharmaceutical salesman met with the doctor.

"These pills just came out. They're amazing. A new miracle drug. They make you feel great."

The doctor looked at the samples that the pharmaceutical salesman had placed in his arms.

"Oh, and I'm legally required to tell you that patients who take this pill will probably die."

"Sorry, what?"

"But otherwise there's no real side effects. Which makes it better than any other antidepressant."

"Wait, but – "

"I hope you'll prescribe this to many patients. It will help them have a quality of life."

"Not if they die!"

"Doc, we'll all die from something sooner or later. The clinical studies say that people die. But people die without taking this pill too. We're all going to die. At least this medicine will improve our quality of life while we're alive."

"You're killing people!"

"And you will too once you learn about the profits. For every dozen prescriptions you hand out you get a free red convertible sports car."

The doctor paused. "Can I get more samples?"

"Sure, I'll bring another box tomorrow."

"I think I know which patients are dumb enough for me to pawn this drug off to."

"The ones who are so messed up that they can't get any worse and are desperately willing to try anything?"

"No. The ones who aren't curious. If you do what you're told without questioning authority, then you'll be victim to any power that wants to control you. But thinking. Questioning. Reflecting on your own instead of just accepting it at face value. There are the thinkers. And then there are the people dumb enough to do something just because someone tells them to."

"Alright, doc. Good luck."

"Oh, I won't need it. I've already got twelve patients who will put any pill in their mouth that I tell them to."

"Then the sports car is yours."

"See you tomorrow."

The doctor met with eleven patients. They all agreed, excited to feel better. But the twelfth patient asked questions.

"What are the side effects?"

"There are very few side effects."

"Are they serious?"

"None of the side effects will hurt."

"But what are they?"

The doctor sighed. Damn these patients who actually think for themselves! Always asking questions about his decisions. This was supposed to be easy to get twelve people to take the pills, but now this last patient is holding out and preventing him from cashing in on his convertible.

"Look, Ken, if you take this pill, I'll give you $1,000."

The patient scratched his head. "Um, why – why would you pay me?"

"Just take the goddamned pill!"

The patient shook his head. "I'm not feeling it, doc."

The doctor took the pill. Swallowed it. And felt much better. And now that he had prescribed twelve pills, his sports car would come tomorrow!

The next day, the pharmaceutical salesman did not come by. Nor the next day. A week went by. "Where's my sports car?!" thought the doctor. He called the pharmaceutical company.

"Oh, didn't you hear? The salesman passed away last week."

"Oh, I'm terribly sorry to hear that," the doctor said.

"Yeah, he had a truckload of Viagra samples and decided to experiment by taking them all at once to impress his wife."

"And did he?"

"He got so big that he exploded and died of blood loss."

"Oh my god!"

"Yeah, those pills were supposed to be by prescription only."

"Well, I'm sorry to hear that."

"Yes."

"Hey, um, by the way, the red sports car that comes when doctors prescribe – "

"Yeah, let me see what I can do for you."

## Luca Bianchi

"Philippe Mercier."

"I'm sorry, how do you spell that?"

"Phee-leep. Weez two pee'z."

"Uh-hun."

"Mer-see-ay. M-E-R. C-I-E-R."

"Great. Philip, we have you scheduled for room 703."

"Where iz zee elevator?"

"To the right. Here's the wifi code."

But Philippe – or should I say Luca Bianchi – was in no need of using the hostel's wifi. He had his own secure hotspot to protect his top secret transmissions back to Rome. He was not a tourist. He was a spy. A specially-trained agent in high-level political espionage. Philippe Mercier had come to Washington, DC to see the Smithsonians. But Luca Bianchi was here to infiltrate the secrets of Congress and undermine Wilson's attack on Germany and Italy. The United States was on the verge of entering the war, and the Central Powers needed all of the advantages they could get.

"Which floor?" the backpacker asked as Luca rolled his suitcase into the elevator.

"Euh, seh-veen."

"Are you French?"

"Yehs."

"Oh, from what city?"

"Uh, from – from Toulouse."

You have to be careful at hostels. There are people there who aren't American and they might actually have heard of a city outside of the U.S. If they ask him questions and he trips up on his fake story, his cover is blown. But this time, Luca is lucky. He's an American.

"Oh, never heard of it."

"Eet eez een zee South of France."

"Ah, ok, near Paris?"

Luca could tell by now that he was talking with an American.

"Kind of."

The elevator reached floor seven. And Luca – I mean Philippe – got out to find his room.

"Eez zees room number seven zéro three?" he asked his roommate.

"Yeah."

"Oh, good. I weel take zees bed."

"Hey, I'm Brian."

"Philippe."

"Nice to meet you."

"Yes, a pleasure."

"Are you from France?"

"Yes, I am."

"I can tell by your accent."

Why had Luca chosen to take a French identity? Surely the French accent is an acquired skill. Why not any other nationality?

"Because zee French lexicon borrows more words from Italian than from any other language."

Luca was a linguist. He was the most brilliant analyst that the Italian External Intelligence and Security Agency had ever known. As an expert in foreign languages, Luca chose French because, well, why not? Picking up that accent should be easy since the languages are so close. And who doesn't love a handsome Frenchman?

The next day Luca got ready. At ten o'clock Congress would be in session. And then the fun begins. He arrived at the Capitol to proceed with his plot.

"I would like a ticket to enter the House gallery."

"You can get one from your embassy."

The French embassy will ask questions since Philippe Mercier does not exist. And the Italian embassy will expose his entire story of why Philippe Mercier needs a ticket for Luca Bianchi with a different name pretending to be French. All this within earshot of American tourists applying for Italian visas.

So instead, Luca did what every spy does when he needs to exchange for a secret commodity on the black market. Craigslist.

Luca posted an ad to buy passes to Congress.

*Looking for extra passes for Congress. My family is from Puerto Rico so we don't have a Congressman to contact to request a tour. Willing to pay $15 or $20 or $1,000 for this pass that you can get for free from your Congressman. Email me at Jorge.Alvarez@gmail.com."*

Luca waited. And waited. Nobody. Not even the Nigerian princes asking for his bank account so they can wire him the money. Finally, one reply.

*Hi Mr. Alvarez, Happy to give you a ticket through my Congressman. You don't need to pay. I have an extra because my aunt won't be joining us for the Capitol tour. She's too tired from walking yesterday. Meet me at the entrance at 10am. I'll give it to you then. – Will*

"Zee Americans are blindly generous. He would give away access to his government's secrets without asking for a penny in exchange."

Luca was at the meeting place. He looked around. Lobbyists in suits and ties discussing a Senator's position. Families with kids and parents in shorts and "I Love DC" t-shirts. U.S. Capitol Police that could thwart Señor Alvarez's exchange and deter Signor Bianchi's plot. Luca waited patiently. He looked at his watch. 10:07am. Congress was now in session. Was this a trap to catch him? Was "Will" coming after all? Luca began to sweat. Those U.S. Capitol police with their guns were one trigger-pull away from assassinating him. After all, he was a foreign enemy in times of war. Should his cover be blown, his life would be in grave danger.

"Mister Alvarez!"

Luca looked up. Will!

An American with his father and two daughters arrived.

"Sorry we're late. Devon needed a diaper change and – "

"No worries. Thanks for your ticket."

"Oh, that's the thing. Um, our toddler ate it."

"What?"

"Yeah, she puts everything in her mouth. When we're traveling it's hard to keep an eye on her. Sorry."

"So you mean ..."

"Yeah. Sorry. But I wanted to come and tell you in person."

Luca's plan was foiled. By a two-year-old. How demeaning. A spy with an international reputation had just had a toddler kick his ass.

"I'll give you $1,000 for one of your passes."

"What?"

"$2,000."

Will scratched his head.

"Are you – "

"I had an important meeting with a Senator and I need to get in."

"But didn't they send you an invitation pass?"

"Yes. My toddler ate it."

The world is run by old people but sometimes it seems that the whim of a toddler has the most control.

Will scratched his head.

"I promised my dad we'd all go to the Capitol tour together. It means the world to him."

Luca glanced at Will's father. 6'2". 364 lb. Shirt size 4XL. His obesity forced him into a wheelchair. Luca paused and brainstormed solutions to the situation as only a spy can contemplate.

Luca glanced up at Will, paused, and then explained a plan.

Will went in with his ticket. His daughter went in with her ticket. Philippe Mercier – I mean Jorge Alvarez – went in with one ticket. And Will's other daughter went in on her grandfather's stomach under his t-shirt. Two entries for the price of one ticket.

"Thank you, Will."

"Hey, no problem. Good luck at your meeting."

And Luca went on to meet and mingle and extract all of the secrets from the House Intelligence Committee. After all, the world was at war. And one single vote could prevent America from entering the war and defeating Italy.

After a day's work, Luca made his way back to the hostel. He sent a cable to Rome with all of the secrets he had unearthed. As he was turning off his hotspot, he went to get coffee. Not coffee but espresso. Italian espresso. He went downstairs to the common room and entered the kitchen.

All of a sudden, his eyes gazed upon the most beautiful lady he had ever seen. He felt the attraction in his heart. His heart skipped a beat. His heart flew to Cloud Nine. His heart raced faster and faster. His heart was full of passion for this gorgeous stranger. As a man, he did the only reasonable thing a man could do: sit at the kitchen counter a few bar stools away from her, drink his coffee and start a conversation.

He fell in love. Head-over-heels. She was the fire in his heart that lit his desire.

"So what do you do for a living?" she asked.

Alas, the fatal question that every spy dreads. Which false identity should he give her?

"If I lie and say a more prestigious career, would you lose all trust?"

"Nobody likes a phony. There's nothing more sexy than being authentic."

"Well, then, I can assure you that I have an exciting, high-paying career. And I'm not lying."

But how long could Luca hold out from disclosing the truth? How many more relationships will suffer from his secret double life? How many more girlfriends and fiancées will dump him for suspected cheating when he goes out at night to meet other people? No, it wasn't worth it for this lady. She was the love of his life. And Luca chose love over his career. He quit his job at the Italian External Intelligence and Security Agency and spent the rest of his days with her, happily ever after.

So what about the War to End All Wars? Italy changed sides to join the allies. Wilson entered the war and defeated the Central Powers. Even though Luca's mission was not carried out, Italy still victoriously won the war. And Luca lived happily ever after.

JOHN R. TEEVAN III

# Dr. God

"Dr. Matthews, this man's life is in your hands," the police officer said as he brought the stretcher to the ER. "He killed a gang member from the opposite gang. Shot him at point blank range. The cold-hearted bastard blew his brains out. Now this murderer is in your hospital for treatment of the fractured limbs and concussion that resulted from the fight. We broke up the fight. Now it's up to you as to whether or not this man lives. He's bleeding profusely and has so many broken bones that he'll probably never be able to walk again. He might have lost his ability to speak after all the traumatic brain injuries he received. What quality of life does he have left? Can't walk. Can't talk. He'll spend the rest of his life in prison mooching off taxpayer expense. He'll probably be a vegetable. If he's lucky he'll die. How much will insurance pay you for all the surgeries to fix him up? Only so he can go to jail and probably commit suicide there. But, Dr. Matthews, you're the ER doctor, not me. I'm just a cop. My job is to bring the criminals to you. And you decide their life or death. So what will it be? Will you let God punish him with death – or will you let the Law punish him with prison for life? This man's life is in your hands. Dr. Matthews, what will it be?"

Dr. Matthews fainted. He was so overwhelmed by the situation that he couldn't take it any longer and passed out. Without the doctor, the murderer died.

But who suffers? Who is punished in this situation? Dr. Matthews certainly was punished: for the rest of his life he has the burden of blood on his hands. Not the usual blood that he gets on his hands during surgery. No, this blood on his hands was metaphysical.

He bears the guilt of having killed a fellow human. Perhaps Dr. Matthews suffers more than his late patient. Yet how is the patient punished? After all, Dr. Matthews and the patient are both murderers. An eye for an eye. The killer was killed. And for the gang member, it was much less painful than life in prison – a vegetable unable to communicate or move. Dr. Matthews was not legally punished for wrongful death – the gang member was a criminal and Dr. Matthews had an untarnished reputation as an asset to the hospital. Why should the hospital side with the killer and not Dr. Matthews?

So how does this story end? It doesn't. Dr. Matthews tended to the next patient in the ER, making his rounds to save lives. And the police officer went back out to the streets to bring in the next criminal. Gang violence is destructive. And sometimes the victims make it to the ER for their judgement before Dr. Matthews before they ever make it to the judge. Sometimes Dr. Matthews decides their life and death before the death sentence is handed down by the judges. In a sense, Dr. Matthews became God – making judgements of who will live and who will die. The police nicknamed him "Dr. God." That's kind of a cool nickname, isn't it? "Dr. God." But considering he was "Dr. God," Dr. Matthews was very humble. "They never told us it would be like this in med school! I was supposed to be doing plastic surgery with a six figure salary, not getting squeamish seeing fractured skulls and holding the awful burden of deciding whether or not someone lives to see tomorrow – or dies in my hands." But each day it was like this. Another ambulance arrived, as the police officer came with the stretcher – filled with blood and painful injuries – and Dr. God fainted.

## The Berlin Wall

Elisabeth. At last. Frank would be reunited with his love. The news made everyone rejoice. The Berlin Wall was coming down. The savage instruments of control – of human containment of ideas – of artificial enemy political boundaries to prevent free thought and brain drain – at last the Berlin Wall was coming down. Germany was reunited. Lands under communist control were freed. And Frank could at last be reunited with his lover.

It had been forty-four years, but to Frank the memory of when he first met Elisabeth seemed like yesterday. He never forgot her. They met in 1945. The Nazis surrendered. Berlin was liberated. And the Americans and Soviets met in Germany to negotiate the new world order. As he celebrated the victory of war, he met Elisabeth. His heart rejoiced upon the sight of her more than it would have rejoiced from conquering the entire known world. She lit up his life and melted his heart.

"What is your name?" Frank asked. But she didn't understand what he was saying. He was an American GI and she was an East German who didn't speak a word of English. But some things in life need no translation. She was more beautiful than words could describe – in any language. They fell in love.

The commander issued the order. The GIs were coming home. The men rejoiced. But not Frank. As East Germany fell to Soviet hegemony, he faced the harsh reality that he might never see Elisabeth ever again. What a terrible curse it is to go home. How he wished he could hide out in Berlin and stay with Elisabeth for the rest of his life. But, alas. An order is an order. Frank never forgot that farewell. They kissed on the platform and embraced as if they would never see each other again. The train whistle blew. And Frank took his bag and boarded the train back west as East Berlin sealed off its borders to the West.

Until today. He would finally get to see her. How he was looking forward to this moment with all his heart. The men brought pick axes and broke up the wall – the symbolic reunification of a divided Germany and the crumbling of the USSR. But it wasn't fast enough. Frank needed to get to his love. With all his might, Frank grabbed blocks of cement with both hands and pushed them aside to clear the way and open the wall.

At last, the wall was penetrated. Frank ran into East Berlin. Elisabeth! Elisabeth! He searched with desperation for his love. Through the streets. To her apartment – he never forgot her address. Hoffmann Street 752, Third Floor in the Bergmannkiez District. And here he was. In front of her door. The Berlin Wall divided them for years, but now only this thin wooden door separated them. All he had to do was knock and they'd be reunited.

Knock, knock.

The door opened.

"Elisabeth!" He could not believe his eyes. She was just as beautiful as he remembered her forty-four years ago. "My dear Elisabeth, how I've missed you!"

"Frank! Oh my god! I haven't seen you in forever. How are you?"

"My dear Elisabeth, I've never forgotten you. After all these years. How I've missed you."

"Me too."

"Oh, Elisabeth, I love you – "

A man came to the door from inside the apartment.

"Frank, this is Hermann."

"Oh, hello. How do you know Elisabeth?"

"I'm her husband. And you?"

Frank was crushed. Betrayed. His heart had been backstabbed. How could she forget him?

But, alas, years and political borders and language and culture separated Frank from his love. How could they be together? How could they possibly *not* be together?

Frank returned home. Broken-hearted. She had moved on. But not him. The die-hard romantic, relishing the past. But memories are always more perfect and more beautiful than the present. Why settle for mediocrity when you can live in the amazing past?

Frank sighed. It was a long flight back across the Atlantic.

Some people move on. Others dwell in the past. Some live in a dream that clouds their present reality. But alas. It takes two to tango. And a love story is never complete without heartbreak.

"So how do you know Frank?" Hermann asked Elisabeth.

"Oh, we used to fool around after the war. But nothing serious."

"And you still remember him forty-four years later?"

"He was good to me."

"But I'm not. You cheated on me by giving your affections to Frank when he knocked on our door. And the penalty for cheating is death. I'll alert the communist authorities and have you stoned. You are impure."

"You can call Stalin all you want, Hermann, but the Berlin Wall came down yesterday. I'm a free woman."

"Then I will beat you like I always do. This time you won't live to tell the tale."

The Soviets had cemented marriage and made divorce illegal. But now there was a power vacuum as the Russian Federation formed and the German Federal Republic reorganized and the Soviets left. And adjudicating a forced marriage between a man who beats his wife and a Soviet law that prevents divorce was the least of their concerns as the heads of state negotiated who should control the Soviet nuclear missile arsenal.

"Screw you, Hermann. I'm a free woman."

And Elisabeth was the first East German to leave East Germany. She took a plane to America and lived a long and happy life with Frank.

So there. Being a romantic does have its use. Living in the past is not a waste of time. And falling in love does have a happy ending.

# The Mechanic

"So you're an auto mechanic?"

"Surgeon."

"What do you mean?"

"I stick my hands into the (auto)body and fix (body) parts that are broken."

"But you work with cars, not humans."

"I improve people's lives by fixing their (auto)body parts."

"But you just fix cars. You have no medical knowledge."

"We do the same thing. Opening up a car is just as dangerous as surgery. The only difference is at the end I have grease on my hands instead of blood."

The florist sighed. He was just talking to a mechanic. Andrew was nothing more than a grease monkey. "Having a doctorate in medicine and having an associate's degree – or an eight-week certificate – in how to change oil are not the same thing."

"Frankenstein didn't have a medical doctorate and he brought dead body parts to life."

"Right, but mechanics don't do that."

The mechanic smiled. "Frankenstein built the monster from grave robbing dead corpses and sewing the body parts together. Likewise, I've been rummaging through junk yards. I have enough parts to build an engine with enough thrust to get us to the moon. The cabin is set – comfortable leather car seats with air conditioning – you'll need the AC for re-entry when you burn up in the atmosphere. I just need an astronaut." The mechanic thought to himself, "I need a test victim – a sacrificial lamb – to see if my rocket will burn to pieces or not on re-entry. And this guy is annoying me so much with his 'You're just a mechanic' questions that I'll pick him." But the mechanic didn't say that. He simply said, "Would you like to be the first florist in space?"

"omg yes!"

"Perfect. Just sign here. Just like when surgeons make you sign a waiver so you can't sue them if you die during their operation, well, being thrust into space at 18,000 mph and re-entering the atmosphere at 3,000°F carries some risk too."

"I'm finally convinced. You are a full-fledged surgeon. If you can get me to the moon, then mechanics have more training than a medical doctor."

"Well, I *think* I can get you to the moon. Just sign here and we'll find out."

## Unwritten Rules

"Objection, your honor! The DA is presenting evidence that was collected *ex legit voca*. That's illegal," said the defense attorney.

"Says who?" demanded the prosecutor.

"Our constitution protects our right against *ex legit voca*."

"Where?"

The judge banged his gavel and called both counsels to his stand. He turned to the defense attorney. "Where the hell does it say that that's illegal?"

"That right is explicitly protected by our constitution."

The judge scratched his head. "But where?"

"What do you mean?"

The judge handed him the 1,891-page archive of legal precedents.

"You find it. And you win this case. I hope you can speed read. I'm recessing this trial for lunch. By the time we return, well, let's just say, you have one hour to read 1,891 pages."

The defense attorney sighed. "Well, at least I packed my lunch today. There's always a long line at the cafeteria." And he saved time by reading while eating.

England's constitution is common law. It's not a written

document that outlines the structure and function and role and limitations of each branch of government. Their constitution is just the legal precedents set over hundreds and hundreds of years stemming from the Magna Carta.

So where does this story take place? Is the trial happening in America that never became independent from England, and is therefore still governed by British Common Law? Is the trial taking place in London? Is the trial taking place in a separate country that has a different legal system ... like, for example, Florina or Movrastan? It doesn't matter. They still have an unwritten constitution. Where's James Madison when you need him?

The fate of this poor criminal hinged on his attorney's ability to find three Latin words in a dense archive. Couldn't he just look the constitution up online and do a Control + F search and find it quickly? No. The legal archives were not online. Court trials from three centuries ago were public record, but they gathered dust at the County Clerk's office. They never saw the light of day. Until today. When an attorney's career and a criminal's life depended on it.

"What does this paragraph even mean? It's all in Latin!" the defense attorney complained. Latin may be a dead language, but it is alive and well in our English legal vocabulary. "If only I had taken Latin instead of Spanish in high school. I though Latin was useless since nobody speaks it. But this could be the deciding factor in whether I win or lose this case. If only I could read this..." But all he could remember was *veni vidi vici*. I came. I saw. I conquered. Julius Caesar. The tyrant who toppled the Roman republic. And it seemed democracy would crumble today, as well, if this attorney could not uphold the constitution.

Well, he lost the case. He couldn't read Latin at a rate of 1,891 pages/hour. He may have lost the battle but he won the war. The defense attorney became the chairman of the very first

Constitutional Convention. He wrote a hard copy of a concise constitution that all could see, honor, protect and uphold. The unwritten constitution became a tangible document that all could access. And instead of the dusty archives at the County Clerk's office, well, he had all of the delegates bring iPads and they combined their drafts on a Google Doc so everyone could edit it. And then they uploaded it to the internet so all could access it. And it was written in a language that all could understand. Rather than formal, stuffy Latin that nobody could make sense of, it was written in English. And the law of The People became the law of The People. And it was accessible to all. And democracy and justice were achieved.

JOHN R. TEEVAN III

## Atomic Secrets[7]

The Soviet rocket scientist met with the covert agent in the café in Berlin. West Berlin? East Berlin? We don't know. That information was classified.

Agent Harderman had bought off one of the rocket scientists working behind the Iron Curtain. Dr. Ivanov had access to the plans for the atomic facility that, among other things, would build nuclear missiles that Moscow would aim directly at Washington, DC. With access to these secret plans, Dr. Ivanov was willing to exchange them for an astronomical sum. The amount Harderman gave Dr. Ivanov was enough dollars to build the entire atomic facility itself. But now without the plans … or the planner: the coffee was poisoned.

Dr. Ivanov dropped his coffee cup and watched it shatter on the floor. With exasperated eyes, he glanced with fear at the agent. "You?- You?-"

"Sorry," Harderman said, as Dr. Ivanov collapsed to the floor. "I had to cover my traces. But keep the money. There's plenty of that where that came from." And the agent took the briefcase with Soviet atomic secrets and walked away.

Taking the train back west, Agent James Harderman kept an extra eye out for followers. For followers from any country. From

---

[7] This piece first appeared in John R. Teevan III, "Atomic Secrets," *A Mysterious Evening in Vienna* (Albany, NY: Self-published; printed by Create Space Independent Publishing Platform, 2017). I am including it here because the new sequel story comes right after.

anywhere. For *everyone*.

In fact, a little bit too *much* of an eye out.

He suddenly gazed upon the most beautiful lady he had ever seen. From head to toe, she was entrancing. All language – and mind you, as a covert operatives agent, he knew quite a few languages – all language was lost from his entranced mind. He dropped his briefcase, which quietly thudded on the floor of the coach heading through Prague. At lightning speed. Things can get overlooked when passing at lightning speed. Including the fact that he had just dropped the briefcase containing papers with atomic secrets that could destroy the world should they fall into the wrong hands. Or, better yet, fall to the floor.

But Agent Harderman was so taken aback by his natural attraction to this woman that he momentarily lost all sense of time, place, perspective and identity. He was not Covert Agent James Harderman of the U.S. CIA. He was a lover and she was his soulmate. And –

Bam! Suddenly the burst of a machine gun struck James, and he fell backwards. Away from her. Away from his future. Away from his love. Away from his briefcase. Away from the papers containing the atomic secrets that could destroy the world.

And he blacked out.

Beep! Beep! Beep! The heart rate monitor was the first thing James heard. He must be in a hospital. Somewhere in Switzerland. And –

Her!! It was the lady on the train! "Where?- Wh-?"

"Sh!" She told him. "They will find you if you make noise! And – "

"Where am I?"

"We're hiding you in my home in Spain. Soviet agents seized the train in Czechoslovakia and shot you."

"And who are you?"

"Maria."

"Are you a spy? A civilian? A Soviet? A NATO operative? A – "

"I am Maria. A Spaniard. Nothing more."

"Can I trust you?" he probed.

"How should I know? Why should I care? How should I know who you choose to trust or not?"

"My briefcase!" Harderman exclaimed as he suddenly realized he was missing the papers that could unleash the plans for an atomic facility.

"Don't worry."

"But – "

"They're in good hands," she reassured.

"Do you have them?"

"They're in good hands."

"But – " he stammered.

"No time for details. We must move on now. Hurry!" And they got into a car and headed for Paris.

Border police. James had bloody bandages wrapped around

his left arm where he had been shot. What will they do?

"Are you together?" asked the border agent.

"Yes," responded Maria.

And they lived the rest of their days together in France.

So how does the story end? Anyone who saves the world from nuclear armageddon deserves a happily ever after. James and Maria got married in Paris. They had an elaborate wedding at the beautiful Notre-Dame Cathedral. To protect their identities they were married under the names on their counterfeit French passports. After a career of killing spies and high-stakes secret nuclear negotiations, James retired to a peaceful life of playing boules in the Jardin du Luxembourg in Paris. Maria wrote adventure novels about falling in love with mysterious spies on trains and the exciting adventures that result from these encounters. She wrote under a pseudonym in her native Spanish so none of her new friends in Paris would know about her past. Maria and James had a long and happy marriage. There was a sense of freedom they won by giving up their previous identities – their past – and living the dream they chose for themselves. They loved each other more and more each day and were forever grateful they met on the train in Prague.

What about the atomic secrets? The briefcase that disappeared on the train? What happened to the papers that could destroy the world?

During the mêlée that ensued during the shooting on the train, the papers were victim of a defenestration. They flew out the window during the chaos. Another Defenestration of Prague[8]. The Soviet Czech civil authorities had over-chlorinated the drinking water. So when the papers reached the gutter, they disappeared in the chlorine-heavy water. Without the plans the atomic facility was never built. Everyone lived happily ever after. Including James and Maria.

---

[8] The word "defenestration" means to throw someone or something out the window. It is a really cool word to write and say, mostly because it is so uber specific in its meaning. In 1618, the Second Defenestration of Prague – where three men were literally thrown out the window – started the Thirty Years' War. While the train carrying James and Maria was passing through Prague, the papers flew out the window. What better occasion to use the word "defenestration"? This could be the Third Defenestration of Prague.

JOHN R. TEEVAN III

# James's Long-Overdue Conversation

Jacques sat on the beach, enjoying the Mediterranean with his wife, Marie. They had moved to Montpellier so they could be half-way between Marie's family in Spain and Jacques's boules tournaments in Paris. Boules, the French version of bocce, was a game that Jacques enjoyed in his retirement. In fact, he was a world champion, playing against old, fat Frenchmen who smoked cigarettes and had not a care in the world. Jacques had not a care in the world, lying on the beach in the South of France. His cell phone rang.

Jacques said « Allô ? »

"James, it's me, Major General –"

Jacques froze. Stunned. They had found him. He dropped his cell phone in the sand. Nobody had called him "James" in thirty years. Not since he was a covert agent. He had carried out many heroic missions that saved the Cold War from exploding. Now he was retired – in hiding – under his French name "Jacques."

"James, can you hear me?"

"Wh- who- who is this?"

"It's Major General Branford."

"Who the hell are you?"

"Remember your old boss, Colonel Baldwin?"

"Yes."

"Well, I'm his successor."

Jacques – who was now James – said, "How did you find me? I'm retired. What blew my cover?"

"James, you're our best spy. You did great at keeping your cover top secret. We searched for you because we need you. Your nation needs you. All of humanity is in danger and we need your help to remove a missile in Russia."

"But the Cold War is over. The Soviet Union dissolved. The threat is a moot point."

"That's exactly the problem, James. All of the warheads are still there. We can't just put them in a recycling bin and be done. This is weapons-grade uranium that could obliterate the world should these missiles fall into the wrong hands. The power vacuum following the collapse of the USSR has only complicated the arms negotiations."

James suddenly remembered last time he engaged in secret atomic negotiations. It was how he met Maria, an encounter that changed his life.

"Where do you need me to go?" James asked.

"Movrastan.[9] A politically-unstable no man's land. Six rival factions are fighting for control. There is no government to negotiate with because anarchy reigns. We can't just send an astronomical sum to a Swiss bank account and have them secretly deliver the warhead to our navy atomic retrieval unit. Here, law and order simply don't exist in Movrastan. There's no organized government to negotiate with. That's one thing I miss about them Commies. At

---

[9] Movrastan is the no man's land mentioned in John R. Teevan III, "International Territory," *A Mysterious Evening in Vienna* (Albany, NY: Self-published; printed by Create Space Independent Publishing Platform, 2017). As described in "International Territory," Movrastan is in political turmoil and not yet diplomatically recognized by the United States.

least the Soviets had an embassy. But this missile in Movrastan could be used as a weapon to threaten the United States into – anything. The Soviets had this missile aimed at New York City – our largest concentration of Americans so they could do the most damage. The codes are still programmed – all they have to do is push the button and millions of lives are lost."

James gasped. He loved to take trips to NYC to sketch at the Met. All of this would be lost with the push of a button.

"Major General Branford, I'll plan to fly to Movrastan tomorrow."

"No, James, we can't do that. Movrastan is not diplomatically recognized by our country. We can't have you meet with their foreign minister. It would contradict our foreign policy to have a U.S. passport-holder recognize their provisional government. Instead, I'll arrange for the Movrastani ambassador to meet you at the U.S. embassy in Armenia."

"I need to get to the heart of the matter as quickly as possible – which means flying into Movrastan. I can't go with my American passport, so I'll go with my French passport."

"James –"

"Call me Jacques."

"But –"

"Don't worry, Major General. I got this one."

"Do you speak Movrastani?"

James – I mean Jacques – paused. "Major General Branford, I am the most skilled linguist the CIA has ever known. I speak, read and write sixteen languages fluently – which is not bad considering

I'm an American. I'll just use Rosetta Stone on the flight over and learn Movrastani. No problem."

"Ok. Report back with updates."

"Over and out."

James approached his lover – his soulmate – his wife. It was that dreaded conversation. He had to leave for his mission. How could he tell her? He never explained to her that he was a retired covert agent. James approached his lover.

"Maria, my dear, there's something I need to tell you. Remember that train ride in Prague when we met?"

She look at him, starry-eyed, and joyfully, dreamily replied, "Of course, James. I've never forgotten that first night we met."

"And remember you hid me when I told you the police were coming after me because of a bad break-up with my ex?"

She nodded.

"And remember I told you we needed to flee to a foreign country and change our names so my crazy ex would stop stalking me?"

"Mm-hmm."

"And remember that briefcase I was so concerned about safekeeping?"

"Yup."

"Well, that wasn't my dissertation in my briefcase. I'm not an assistant professor. I'm a covert agent for the CIA. That briefcase contained atomic secrets that could destroy the world. Our safety is in peril again, and I need to step away from my retirement to diffuse another nuclear threat. I may or may not return home. If I die, I will love you with all my heart, all my mind and all my soul. Maria, I love you."

Maria paused. James waited for her response. He had just dumped his deepest, darkest secret onto her. He had lied, and now – was she ready for the truth? Would she ever love him again? Would she know what to believe?

Maria sighed, then said, "Well, that's a relief. I had no idea you were a spy. I suppose I owe it to you to tell you this. I'm not a nurse. I nursed you back to health when you were shot in Prague. I bandaged your wounds and treated your injuries. But nursing is only a hobby. My childhood dream of becoming a nurse was interrupted when my career began. I am a spy. I am in the EU's counter-terrorism division."

James's jaw dropped.

"I told you I was a Spaniard. Which I am. But my family is Movrastanian immigrants. Growing up in Barcelona with Spanish, Catalan and Movrastani spoken at home, I soon learned to be fluent in so many languages that I became the EU's counter-terrorism polyglot. It all stems from my love of speaking Movrastani."

"You speak Movrastani?!"

"I read, write and speak it fluently."

"That's it! We're going to Movrastan. I need your help."

"James, should I bring my Spanish passport?"

"Call me Jacques. We'll bring our French passports."

"I have a feeling we have a lot to catch up on," Maria said.

"It'll be a long flight. We can talk. But not in English – or

JOHN R. TEEVAN III

Spanish – or French – do you speak Icelandic?"

"Fluently."

"Then we'll fill each other in about our espionage careers. But we'll do it in a language that nobody else will understand."

"Sounds good, James – I mean Jacques."

# President McClellan

*Abraham Lincoln is a hero of mine. He was able to unite people from diverse backgrounds into one – such as his cabinet of former enemies/rivals – and his success in uniting a divided nation. I admire him for all that he achieved, including saving the union and freeing the slaves. Today Lincoln is honored as having been our best president. But when he was in office he was hated. The South hated Lincoln because he was invading their country and killing them. And the North hated him because their sons were getting sent off to die in the bloodiest war in our nation's history. And there was no end in sight to the war. Lincoln was never popular until he was assassinated. Then everyone felt bad for him. In fact, when Lincoln was running for re-election, he was predicted to lose in a landslide. George McClellan was a Union general who was so incompetent that he lost almost every battle in the most important, strategic region right near the U.S. capital. Lincoln fired McClellan. The Democrats nominated McClellan for president in 1864 on a platform to end the war by letting the South secede. So it was Lincoln vs. McClellan for president. And the incompetent, loser general was predicted to defeat Lincoln in a landslide.*

*Then William Tecumseh Sherman led his March to the Sea and Atlanta fell and Northern voters realized they would win the war. And Lincoln won his re-election. Slavery was abolished. And the union was re-unified. All because the attack on Atlanta was successful. But what if Sherman lost that battle? McClellan would have been elected. This story is what would have happened in that scenario.*

Lincoln was voted out. His life's work to free the slaves and save the union was all a waste. And the war cost a fortune in money and hundreds of thousands of lives. A human life is priceless. Now the blood of hundreds of thousands of Americans was on his hands. Lincoln went down in history as the worst president, not the best president. There was no Lincoln Memorial. Pennies and $5 bills did not have Lincoln on them. Lincoln was at best forgotten and at worst remembered as the worst president in history who aimlessly started a bloody, destructive war that nearly ruined his country. Poor Abe.

As soon as McClellan took office, he diplomatically recognized the South. The war was over. Everyone went home.

The North and South never reunited. Today, U.S. passports begin with Lincoln's quote, "and that government of the people, by the people, for the people, shall not perish from the earth." But it did. It crumbled. The country split in two. Instead of having Lincoln – who was now the worst president in history – on the front page of the U.S. passport, it now said "United States of America. Not to be confused with the Confederate States of America."

The South was now independent. This was exactly what the French and British needed. The Industrial Revolution thirsted for cotton. And as soon as the Civil War ended, the union naval blockade was lifted. The British traders came. And bought cotton. And bought more cotton. "Hey, I wonder if we can get better rates if we colonize the South?" Queen Victoria commented to Emperor Napoléon III. Soon the British navy was outside Richmond. The French had already occupied Mexico. Maximilian I sent in his forces to Texas. "Help!!" cried Jefferson Davis. He telegraphed his former alma mater, U.S. Military Academy at West Point, asking for military support.

"Sorry, brother, you got your own gig now. You wanted out. Don't come crying to us now."

At this time, the British had the best navy in the world and the French had the best army in the world. And the South was exhausted from the destruction of the Civil War. Not wanting another conflict, the Confederacy became a banana republic – a colony – of the British and French. Anything they wanted, the South gave. Rather give them money than have bloodshed. And, after all, the rich white Southerners were signing treaties giving away their cotton, but they weren't losing anything. Because the slaves were doing the work. The British and French had abolished slavery on their mainland, so this was the lucrative offshore labor their textile industry needed to produce the cotton. The French and the British shared the South – their colony – like spheres of influence in China. Each occupied a specific region while still allowing local authorities to act with their European colonizers.

Then the Berlin Conference happened. While negotiating the Scramble for Africa, Bismarck burst out: "But what about the Confederate States of America?! We should establish rules for colonizing that territory too!"

President Davis sent a desperate telegraph to President McClellan. "Help! All of Europe is coming to exploit us! The U.S. issued the Monroe Doctrine. Now we need your help in enforcing it. I propose a joint declaration between the USA and the CSA. We will unite against a European invasion."

U.S. Secretary of State John Quincy Adams replied, "I wrote the Monroe Declaration as a unilateral declaration, not a bilateral declaration. The Brits wanted in on it, but I said no. It gives more autonomy for our country to be able to make its own decision. Jeff, you left the union, so you left our protection. You made a decision, now live with it. Peace out!"

And the North built a wall along the Mason-Dixon Line. Once the French and British and Germans invade the South, well, just like Trump's wall, they didn't want people coming north into the United States.

Historians often say that slavery – and the resulting rich-poor gap – led to the fall of Rome when the Huns invaded. Likewise, slavery – and the resulting rich-poor gap – led to the fall of the Confederacy when the European powers invaded.

Napoléon III retook New Orleans and the Louisiana Purchase. "I am taking back what is rightfully mine," he said in a French accent. And the Mexicans took back the Mexican Cession. "We may have lost the Mexican-American war, but this is round two!"

As the South fell apart and the British navy began unloading redcoats, there was a mass exodus of Southerners trying to flee the South and head north. "Mister Gorbachev, tear down this wall!" Jefferson Davis demanded.

"Hey, you wanted out. You made your decision, now live with it," McClellan replied, and then sealed the gates, locked the doors and fortified the wall with infantry.

Slaves fled north, forming lines at the border. Slaves were granted refugee status and admitted to the North. They sought political asylum from a system that exploited human slavery. The Underground Railroad became a paved highway to Freedom, and many slaves fled north.

Chaos, war and destruction plagued the South, and it appeared the United States would never be reunited. "What a disaster, Mister President," moaned Secretary of State John Quincy Adams. "The whole southern half of our country has fallen into crisis."

"You don't understand," replied McClellan. "I'm a political genius. Wait until they're at their weakest point. Then call Jeff Davis. He'll come crying back to the Union. And we haven't lost a single drop of Northern blood during my administration."

"That'll never work."

McClellan picked up the phone and dialed Davis's cell phone.

"Hello Jeff, this is –"

"We're in. We agree. Just get that ratified through Congress ASAP so we can be readmitted before this debacle gets worse."

"And you'll – "

"Yes, we'll abolish slavery. You Yankees win. Just get us out of this quagmire! S.O.S.!"

And the Civil War ended. John Quincy Adams re-issued his Monroe Doctrine, this time called the McClellan Doctrine.

"I do all the work. When will I ever get one of my doctrines named after me?" Adams moaned.

McClellan turned to Adams. "Dude, you're a Federalist. Be lucky I haven't fired you yet," the Democrat barked.

And Germany, France and Britain were kicked out of the South. It is amazing what can be achieved when different people from different backgrounds come together. The North and South, uniting together to combine forces, repelled European intervention in the Western Hemisphere.

The U.S. was reunited. The wall along the Mason-Dixon

Line was ceremonially taken down like the Berlin Wall.

And the American coins were printed with *e pluribus unum*: from many one.

# Bibliography

Delperrié de Bayac, Jacques. *Histoire du Front Populaire* (Paris: Fayard, 1972).

Paine, Thomas. "The American Crisis." *The American Crisis.* (1776). University of Groningen. http://www.let.rug.nl/usa/documents/1776-1785/thomas-paine-american-crisis/chapter-i---the-american-crisis---december-23-1776.php.

Teevan, John R., III. "Atomic Secrets." *A Mysterious Evening in Vienna* (Albany, NY: Self-published; printed by Create Space Independent Publishing Platform, 2017).

Teevan, John R., III. "International Territory." *A Mysterious Evening in Vienna* (Albany, NY: Self-published; printed by Create Space Independent Publishing Platform, 2017).

Teevan, John R., III. "The Spy's White Dress." *A Mysterious Evening in Vienna* (Albany, NY: Self-published; printed by Create Space Independent Publishing Platform, 2017).

Wilson, Woodrow. "The Challenge Accepted: President Wilson's Address to Congress, April 2, 1917." (speech, Washington, DC, April 2, 1917). British Library. https://www.bl.uk/collection-items/president-woodrow-wilsons-address-to-congress-2-april-1917.

JOHN R. TEEVAN III

# About the Author

John R. Teevan III is a writer, traveler, dreamer and artist. He is the author of seven books of historical fiction, romance, spy fiction and comedy. *The Flight Attendant* (2020) was #1 on Amazon's list of bestselling new releases in its genre.

When he's not writing, John loves to draw, travel the world, meet new people, learn foreign languages and experience foreign cultures.

John completed a Bachelor's Degree in French, graduating *summa cum laude* from the Honors College of the University at Albany, State University of New York. John is a member of the Phi Beta Kappa Honor Society. He studied abroad in Paris at France's prestigious Sorbonne University. John went on to complete a Master's Degree in French from the University at Albany, SUNY. He later completed another Master's Degree in Teaching English to Speakers of Other Languages from the University at Albany, SUNY.

In addition to his career as an author, John works at a university. He lives in the Albany, New York area.

John would love to hear from you: AuthorJohnTeevan@gmail.com

For more information, visit: www.AuthorJohnTeevan.weebly.com

# Also by this Author

*The Flight Attendant* (2020) is a collection of short stories that take place at an airport.

*America Invades Canada Again* (2019) is a historical satire.

*Secret Weapon and Last Hope* (2019) is a political drama about power, betrayal, love, oppression, hope amidst adversity, and the forces that build a nation – and prevent its utter demise.

*The Traveler's Sketchbook* (2018) is a collection of John's favorite drawings from his travels around the world.

*The Love Letter with a Bullet Hole* (2018) is a story of two spies who fall in love but cannot be together because they are on opposite sides of the Cold War.

*A Mysterious Evening in Vienna* (2017) is a collection of short stories that capture the essence of adventure, foreign espionage, love, travel and political intrigue. *A Mysterious Evening in Vienna* was # 2 on Amazon's list of bestselling new releases in its genre.

All of John's books are available on Amazon and Kindle.

Made in the USA
Middletown, DE
21 July 2020